RETRIBUTION TRAIL

When ex-army doctor Cass Warton visits his brother Steve's family on their Montana ranch, Kingfisher Blue, the chief of a local band of Cheyenne, comes to ask Cass for his help. Cass goes to the Cheyenne village and saves the life of the chief's wife during a difficult birth. But while Cass is away, his brother's ranch is raided by a gang of cut-throats. Steve is brutally murdered and Annie and her children kidnapped. Together with Kingfisher Blue, Cass sets off on an unrelenting quest for revenge . . .

TEX LARRIGAN

RETRIBUTION TRAIL

Complete and Unabridged

LINFORD
Leicester

First published in Great Britain in 2001 by
Robert Hale Limited
London

First Linford Edition
published 2002
by arrangement with
Robert Hale Limited
London

British Library CIP Data

Larrigan, Tex
    Retribution trail.—Large print ed.—
Linford western library
    1. Western stories
    2. Large type books
    I. Title
    823.9′14 [F]

    ISBN 0–7089–9933–6

Published by
F. A. Thorpe (Publishing)
Anstey, Leicestershire

Set by Words & Graphics Ltd.
Anstey, Leicestershire
Printed and bound in Great Britain by
T. J. International Ltd., Padstow, Cornwall

This book is printed on acid-free paper

1

Young Tim Warton staggered across the yard with a slopping pig pail in each hand. He was whistling a little tune and he smiled as he heard the old sow and her litter squeal in reply as they snuffled on the other side of the pigsty door.

He liked pigs. They were amusing and easy to train. Just as good as any dog, he thought as he opened up and moved carefully against eight small pink bodies towards the long trough.

He looked at them with pride. They were firm-bodied and even the runt was growing fast. Pa had promised the wreckling for himself if he made a good job of rearing the rest. The little fellow would be his very own and the first animal he'd owned in all his fourteen years.

It made him feel like a man. It also made it justifiable that he should now carry a handgun. Uncle Cass had today presented him with an old Army Colt .38 that he'd used during the war which he swore he'd never used in anger. But then, Uncle Cass had been an army doctor and only carried the gun as a last protection because his field hospital was often based dangerously near Rebel lines.

He was proud of Uncle Cass and it was always a red-letter day when he visited them at the remote hill farm in Montana. He told a stack of tales, some harrowing and some heroic but all making Tim wish he was away from the quiet backwoods and seeing some action.

He rushed the feeding of the pigs, wanting to get back to the cosy fireside where Uncle Cass was entertaining his brother, Tim's pa, his ma and Tim's brother and sister.

He took a cursory look around in the corral where the half-dozen mustangs ran free. They were a little restless and the black stallion, leader of the small herd, kept snorting and flinging up his head and listening; just as if he could sniff strange horses around, Tim thought with a frown.

Strange horses could mean strangers. Their small ranch was in a valley surrounded by what were known as the Black Hills of Dakota. He looked around at the distant hills, then he saw the lone figure on horseback silhouetted against the rapidly darkening sky.

His heart seemed to leap within his chest. He knew what it meant to see a lone observer. There would be other men on the other side of those hills.

He also knew that the horseman would be Indian. The Cheyenne were proud. They reckoned they were the true custodians of the land and refused to sneak up on the white settlers. It was well known that the Cheyenne in these parts only showed interest when they had a good reason. The real danger came from the wandering gangs of ex-army soldiers, trained to kill and now homeless. They came upon settlers unawares, looted and destroyed and rode off again when they'd had their fun with the womenfolk.

Suddenly Tim was galvanized into action. Throwing down his empty buckets he ran into the small log cabin, face red and gasping with excitement.

'Pa! There's an Indian standing on Eagle's Point and watching us!' Uncle Cass and Pa grabbed their rifles and came out on to the veranda of the small cabin and looked towards the Point.

Now there wasn't only one Indian; as Pa counted he saw a row of at least ten or twelve. They were easily seen as the setting sun showed red behind them turning them into sharp black figures.

Cass Warton watched coolly. He wasn't a man easily fazed by what he saw. Now he squinted into the setting sun and announced quietly,

'They're not painted up for war and I never heard any rumours about any uprisin's. Mebbee they want to trade hosses.'

Pa Warton shook his head.

'They got their own herds and ours are hardly worth rustlin' never mind tradin' for.'

Pa Warton glanced at Tim and jerked his head towards the door.

'Get inside, son and help your ma with Jess and Bobby. We'll wait here for the varmints if they decide to come on down.'

'But Pa,' Tim said eagerly, 'I got me a gun now, Pa. I can stay and help.'

'You heard what I said, boy! Get inside!'

Tim, recognizing the tone of voice before his pa took off his belt, did as he was told. He felt humiliated and belittled. Hell! He was nearly as tall as his pa! A bit thinner, what his ma called gangly, but he could have pulled a trigger and it would help if there was going to be trouble.

The brothers watched the long still line of warriors. Were they coming on down or were they out assessing the livestock or waiting for reinforcements?

Cass spat on the hard-packed earth

in front of the veranda, his eyes assessing their defences, which were not very much. How many times had he told Steve to build a barricade along the front of the house? But Steve had been easy.

'Who would want to come up here causing mayhem? We aren't worth the effort of ridin' all the way up into the mountains for,' he would say. 'The Cheyenne have been quiet in these parts for years.'

'There's always a first time,' Cass had protested, but Steve accused him of being a scaremonger.

Now it damn well looked as if they were going to be in big trouble.

★ ★ ★

Kingfisher Blue glanced at his brother-in-law, Black Lynx, a man much older than himself and a noted medicine man.

'Well? Do you think he is down there? They see us and are waiting.'

6

Black Lynx looked sullen.

'It is your enterprise. You are the one who does not believe that the Great Spirit will end Moonstone's travail. I say that if we go back she will be delivered. She has fought long and hard. The Great Spirit will reward her efforts. Also the bones tell of good fortune.' He fingered the leather bag of charms about his neck.

Kingfisher Blue wasn't listening to him. He was trying to identify the man with the rancher Steve Warton, but the stranger had his wide-brimmed hat pulled well down over his forehead.

He thought of Moonstone. This birth was not going as the first two births had gone. He'd read the signs in her face that the Spirit of the Underworld had already touched her and his own spirit was crying out to her to have courage and fight on . . .

Black Lynx waited. Would Kingfisher Blue give the order and ride boldly down into the white man's yard, intent on finding the man he was looking for?

Black Lynx reflected on this man he'd heard so much about and a great jealousy stirred within him. Was he not the official medicine man of their village? It was an insult to him to go beyond his judgement. He waited.

Then Kingfisher Blue made his mind up. He had to *know*. He glanced behind him at the waiting men and then nodded. He was ready.

The bronze faces showed no emotion. Kingfisher Blue felt proud. They were ready to obey, but he sensed Black Lynx's fury and resentment. But what did it matter as long as Moonstone's life was saved. He must find the man who'd saved his own leg all those years ago when he was but an unfledged youth seeking to make his first kill to prove himself a man. He'd been gored by a rampant buffalo enraged because her calf was in danger.

He had to find that man for Moonstone.

His moccasined feet urged his pony forward and they began the long slow trek down into the valley. They were an impressive sight, the young dog soldiers following their young chief, and it struck chill into the hearts of Annie Warton and young Tim looking through the window of the log cabin and watching them come.

Annie drew her two younger children to her and they sensed her fear and began to cry. Tim, frightened but trying not to show it, was torn between defending his mother and his siblings and wanting to go out on to the veranda and show his pa and his uncle that he was not afraid.

'Ma, don't cry. Perhaps I should go outside and help Pa and Uncle Cass . . . '

'No!' gasped Annie, panic-stricken. 'Stay with us! If anything happens to Pa and Cass you would be here to shoot us! Promise me you'll shoot us all if we're overrun!'

Tim looked appalled.

'But Ma . . . '

'Promise!' yelled Annie, shivering

violently. 'I've heard what they do to white women . . . Or give me the gun and I'll shoot you all.' She held out her hand for Tim's gun which he held slackly in his hand. Jess started to howl. Annie slapped her firmly on the cheek and she subsided, snuffling into her mother's skirt, while Bobby sat holding their mongrel puppy tightly.

Outside, Steve and Cass watched the small party pick their way slowly down the hillside.

'What should we do, Cass? Give 'em a warning shot over their heads to stop 'em in their tracks? You're the one who's experienced in fighting with the military.'

'I'm not an Indianfighter, Steve,' Cass answered sharply. 'I think a shot would anger them. They look peaceful at present.'

'I don't like the look of 'em. Sly bastards can come all peaceful like and be on us before we could draw breath. I say we should show them some strength.'

10

Steve lifted his rifle for a warning shot but Cass pushed the barrel down.

'Wait!'

'But Cass, we've Annie and the kids to think about!'

'I said wait. I have a feelin' about that feller in front. I seem to remember that plumage he's wearing. Kingfisher feather instead of the usual eagle's feather. It reminds me . . . ' Then he stopped as the party came closer and he could distinguish features, the carved beak-like nose and strong chin, the coarse black hair plaited and bound with rawhide and the Kingfisher feather tucked into a headband at that certain angle . . .

Then Cass let out a great laugh, flung up his hands and to Steve's amazement jumped down from the veranda. Ignoring the rickety steps he made a run towards the incoming party. He took off his hat and waved.

'Kingfisher Blue! By all that's holy, you gave us all a fright! Where in hell have you come from?'

The leading Indian's face split into a wide grin as he spurred his horse forward; then coming at a fine lick he reached down and swung Cass up beside him. For several moments Cass swung high into the air before the pony stopped and Kingfisher Blue let Cass down gently.

Then the Indian was off the pony and hugging the older man as if he were his father.

'I knew I should find you. We have been trailing you for days and always we were a day behind you. I need your help, Man of the Magic Fingers. Oh, yes, I need your help badly.'

Behind them, Steve stared and put down his rifle. The door opened and Annie appeared with the children. She looked, fascinated, at the encounter between Cass Warton and the young chief, while Black Lynx and the rest of the dog-soldiers silently watched the strange little scene.

Then Kingfisher Blue remembered his escort. He turned and waved and they all relaxed. Black Lynx joined his brother-in-law and held up a hand in peaceful greeting.

'You are the one my brother talks about? The one who saved his leg from the rotting disease?'

Cass glanced at a shining-eyed Kingfisher Blue.

'Yeah. Blue was dyin' right hard when I found him. Got mauled by a mother buff and we fought three days to save that there leg. But we did it! How's it been, Blue?'

'As good as new, Magic Hands. A bit stiff at first but now I can cling to a pony's back and shoot from under his belly as well as the strongest youths in our village!' He spoke proudly, then his face changed to a great sadness. 'I want you to ride back with us. It is my wife, Moonstone. Her time is not yet but the papoose wants to break free and is giving her a lot of pain. Black Lynx here has done the best he can. Given her herbal draughts, but they only make her sick. Will you help her?' His dark eyes

13

implored and Cass had no choice.

'Of course I'll do what I can. How far away is your village?'

'Through the pass and a day's ride beyond the hills.'

'Then we must start at once.'

Annie bustled forward.

'Not before you've all eaten, you won't! The very idea!' and she caught the eye of a young Indian standing by the Indian ponies. 'You there, get your brothers to find wood and we'll build a fire outside, and Tim, you go get that side of pork . . .'

'But, Ma, that was set aside for winter,' Tim protested.

'Never you mind about that! Better to feed these men and show friendship than save a side of bacon!'

Tim hurried away to the curing-shed while Annie got out her huge enamel bowl and tipped half a sack of flour into it and proceeded to make the usual panbread for the hungry men.

Soon, coffee was bubbling away, a huge skillet was frying thick slices of pork and Annie was turning out rounds of flat bread as fast as she could make them.

She was surprised. These Indians acted very much like white boys and waited in line for mugs of coffee with not a hint of savagery in them. To think she'd gone into spasms, thinking she could be raped and murdered along with her children, and here was one chucking Jess under the chin and laughing with her! Life held many surprises, even in these backwoods!

They did not stay long after the meal was over. Kingfisher Blue was in a hurry to go home. Steve and Annie and Tim and the two youngsters waved them away sadly. It would have been nice to have more time to talk with the Cheyenne. Tim was quite impressed. These Indians had been so very different from those he had heard about in tales of Indian atrocities.

He heard his father ask Uncle Cass if he knew where they were heading. Uncle Cass's reply had been vague.

'A day's march beyond the pass. In a canyon the Indians call the Home of the White Buffalo.'

'You'll come back here before you move on?'

'Of course. Don't worry about me. I'll be back.' He'd hitched the large black bag of what Tim termed 'Uncle Cass's Mysteries' higher on to the cantle of his horse and rode off with Kingfisher Blue.

The days that followed seemed humdrum to Tim. He fed the pigs and did his daily chores with his pa; he bullied Bobby a little because he thought the lad a bit of a mummy's boy, and he played with Jess, but all the while he wondered just how Uncle Cass was getting on and whether the Indian chief's wife was cured of whatever had ailed her.

He wondered when Uncle Cass would come down the trail and stay with them again. He hoped it would be soon.

2

Mitch Delaney, one-time Major Mitchel Delaney in the Union Army and now the notorious Mitch Delaney wanted by the same army with a thousand bucks on his head, surveyed the scene before him as his men finished searching the ranch house and the buildings grouped around it.

The ranch's small remuda of horses was already loaded down with loot that the men had gathered to take on their journey down into Mexico. It was mainly food, dried staples, some boxes of ammunition and several useful-looking rifles.

He bared his teeth in a grin.

'That's it, boys. Don't get too carried away. Be sensible and only take what's necessary. We burn the rest!'

Ned Scoggins held up a pair of women's drawers.

'I thought I'd pack these and find me a woman they'd fit!' he chortled.

'Get your mind off women, Ned. Remember, we've a long way to go and the army scouts don't give up easy!'

'Yeah, well we got well ahead. No sign of 'em yet, boss. We'll make the border, no sweat!'

Mitch Delaney wasn't so sure. It had been a mistake to raid that last train and take off the army payroll. They should have stuck to civilian trains. It had been a tactical error, but once the boys had seen those strongboxes, there would have been no stopping them. Now, each man had his own share of that payroll stashed in his saddlebags and was responsible to himself only for its safety.

That fact had made them all uneasy. Now they were not trusting each other. Tempers were sharp and Mitch had made his mind up that once over the border, he was going to cut loose and leave the bastards. He kept his mouth shut and not even Jack Stacy, his sergeant all through the war and the man he trusted the most, knew of the plan. He would miss Jack but that was life. He'd seen a certain look in Jack's eyes when he thought he was not being observed. Jack would backshoot him if the situation arose just as he would backshoot Jack in the same circumstances. Mitch was under no illusions. The men followed him because he was the one who could plan and, up until now, his plans had succeeded.

That last raid had had the makings of disaster, but the slow thickheads amongst them had not twigged the danger yet. Jack could be the one to wake up to what was happening back along the trail and when he did, then fireworks could start.

He was not going to stay around to be backshot and robbed. He took a double payout for being boss and what he carried in his saddlebags could set a man up for life.

Now he was in a hurry to get away from this remote ranch. Once the raid was reported, then the military would have the advantage again.

'Fire the ranch and the barns. Leave no traces. If there's anyone hidin' out, then they'll come runnin' if their hide's on fire!' He laughed savagely and watched as several of the men rode around the dilapidated buildings, throwing lighted torches at the dry woodwork. Soon all the buildings were ablaze, smoke and flames curling up into the sky.

'Right! Now load up what you want and let's be away.' He ignored the still bodies of the rancher and his cowhands as if they did not exist.

He was conscious again of the thrill of victory that he'd first experienced during the fighting against the Rebels all those years ago. His jaw tightened when he thought of the court martial he'd suffered after it was all over. To be accused of war crimes! Everyone knew that atrocities had been carried out on both sides! It was to be expected in wartime. The ungrateful bastards in

Washington had used his expertise when it suited them and booted him out of the army like some old rubbish when they didn't require his services any more! They had not even taken into account his own sacrifices. He'd lost his wife and family to the Rebels and his own land had become derelict and then overrun by dirtfarmers. The insult had been too much.

He'd escaped. He wasn't going to break stones for the rest of his life in no penitentiary. No sir! Better be an outlaw. At least he was free.

The bitterness had eaten into him. Now, he knew he'd gone too far down the trail to perdition to change. He knew he was more animal than human and didn't care. The important thing was survival.

They rode out, leaving the burning buildings and dead livestock along with the bodies of the rancher and his crewmen. Vaguely he wondered whether there would be a wife somewhere, perhaps visiting town or a near neighbour. If so, she was going to have a pleasant surprise when she returned . . . He laughed as he rode away.

Ned Scoggins gave him a side glance as they rode together, the men falling in behind them. Mitch didn't like Ned's brash way of assuming second in command, and neither did Jack, who rode close behind.

Sometimes it amused Mitch to see Jack glower and he encouraged Ned, but most times he kept the peace between them, especially before a raid. He didn't want explosions of temper then for it was crucial that everyone knew exactly what their part in the plan was. Each man had his place and they must work as a team. It was like the discipline learned in the army.

Mitch Delaney made sure they all knew that he was still their major and the boss.

It had become increasingly hard riding south, making detours around towns and living off their hard-tack rations and the men were now grumbling that they needed liquor and women. Tension was getting high and Mitch knew that they must have a break soon. Even he was having withdrawal symptoms. His throat was on fire and his guts ached for a long drink of rotgut whiskey, and as for a woman, he would have paid any old hag for a quick poke.

They came to a lonely way station. It wasn't much. Just an agency for changing horses for the once weekly coach service which wasn't due for another three days. Startled, the owner looked up as Mitch strode in followed by his men. The man's arms shot up into the air as Mitch nonchalantly waggled his Colt at him.

'Any women around here?'

The man shook his head so hard it was in danger of falling off. He swallowed a large lump in his throat.

'I do the cookin' and see to the hosses. I've got whiskey.' He smiled a tremulous smile and looked from one to another for approval.

Mitch cursed and the men grumbled.

'Goddammit! You should have a woman doin' the cookin', but let's have the liquor. We're all dyin' of thirst!'

The little man pulled out several bottles from under the counter top and placed them in a row.

'These are all I've got. You're welcome to them.' His smile wavered as he didn't seem to get a friendly response. 'You want food? I'll cook for you. I got beans and pork. It won't cost you much . . . ' His voice died away as Mitch laughed and twisted the top off a bottle, put it to his mouth took a swig and then passed the bottle to Jack while the other men grabbed the rest and drank.

The little man watched his whiskey disappear in a flash.

'Wait,' he cried, 'are you goin' to pay me?'

Mitch thrust his head close to the man's face and grinned, his teeth showing in a wolfish snarl.

'Yes, we'll pay you.'

The man looked relieved until Mitch said in a deadly quiet voice, 'With your life. You can have your life, mister. How's that?' The man's teeth chattered. Then Mitch's fingers caught his shirt collar and twisted and pulled him nearly over the counter. The man could smell the whiskey on Mitch's breath.

'Now bring out your beer pronto. We aim to drink this place dry!'

He shoved the man violently away, making him collide with a stack of tin plates on a shelf, bringing them clattering to the ground.

Hours later they left, singing crude army songs, the little man strung up from one of his own beams and his dead eyes staring into space. There were no witnesses. But the army scouts who came later read the signs. They were well on the track of Mitch Delaney and his band of cut-throats.

Days later, when their food was getting short and there had been several gruelling days of hard riding, they came to the trail leading up into the mountains. Now some of the horses were lame and growing gaunt with hard usage. The men too rode silently, conscious of blisters on arses and between the thighs. They were conscious of their own stink and one of their number was feverish from an earlier wound that refused to heal.

Mitch reined in his mount and rubbed his bristly chin, surveying the range of hills and the narrow trail leading upwards.

'Mebbee we should hide out in the hills until the heat is off,' he muttered to Jack Stacy. Jack Stacy was uneasy. Young Knobby Bowles had joined them just a couple of hours ago. He'd doubled back to take a recce and had returned with the disturbing news that a great cloud of dust hung over the horizon and he was sure it was from a full platoon of soldiers on their track.

'It could be a mistake,' Jack said carefully. Mitch Delaney didn't like any opposition to his ideas. 'We're nearly out of grub and we need to push on as fast as possible.'

'We can't go on without some rest. One of the horses collapsed back there and those bastards will surely find it and guess what's happened. It will happen again. We've got to disappear and the only way we can do it is to get off the beaten track and go cross-country.'

'But it's all strange ground. We don't know where we're headin',' Jack growled.

'We'll have to take a chance. I've always won out in the end, haven't I? We've been through some sticky patches and luck's always been on my side. It'll happen again.'

Jack spat on the ground, his throat dry. He could have killed for a mug of coffee.

'Mebbee your luck ran out when we robbed the military train. I been thinkin', boss, it wasn't such a clever move!'

Mitch stared at him steadily, his eyes icy.

'You keep that thinkin' to yourself, Jack, or there could be trouble.'

'Meanin'?'

'Just what I say. I don't want the rest of the boys thinkin' along those lines.'

'They'll think of them sooner or later.'

'Well, until they do, you keep your mouth shut. D'you hear?'

'And if I don't?' Now Jack sounded truculent.

'Even the most loyal of men could have an accident!'

Jack stared at him for a long moment and then jerked savagely at his horse's mouth, turned and rode down the line of men.

'Right, boys! We're goin' up into the mountains. The boss thinks it's time to find us a hideaway and relax and tend our blistered arses! Now, at the double, let's see what's over the other side of those hills!'

The trail was rough and steep and

wound around boulders and stands of trees. One horse collapsed and died where it lay and another, carrying a load it wasn't used to, slithered over some loose scree and rolled down into an unseen crevice, scattering a couple of boxes of ammunition and a long box containing six new military rifles.

Mitch cursed and bawled to the men to have a care and watch the pack-horses. He was beginning to doubt the wisdom of riding up into the mountainous country. It was deceptive. The only thing that cheered him was the fact that the ground they covered was hard and, if they rode carefully, they would leave no sign behind them. Two men were assigned to follow the main group, dragging branches with plenty of foliage to obliterate any tell-tale signs. Mitch Delaney knew full well how skilled the Indian scouts were when following a red-hot trail.

Then, just as Mitch was about to despair at ever finding somewhere to hide they rode out to face a vista that warmed their hearts. They were on a hill overlooking a verdant green valley in the middle of which was a small ranch with a small herd of horses in the corral close by.

Mitch laughed and looked at Jack, as he raised his ex-army glasses to his eyes.

'You see, Jack, The Delaney luck still holds! There's not a damn cowboy in sight! I bet we've got some poor grubber eking out a livin', growin' vegetables and enjoyin' a nice free life away from wars and civilization! I bet the bastard doesn't even know there's been a war goin' on these last few years! Let's go and visit and teach him the facts of life!'

Jack Stacy grinned and those nearby who heard Mitch's words laughed too.

'Let's hope there's some womenfolk down there to liven things up!' someone said and whooped with a sudden rise of excitement.

Suddenly all the men were imagining women's soft breasts and shapely legs. Blistered arses were forgotten as the sap rose in all of them. It had been a long time . . .

Whooping and shouting as if drunk with liquor they kneed their horses and charged downhill, oblivious to rabbit holes or loose stones in their eagerness to be first in the ranch yard.

Steve Warton heard the drumming hoofs. He paused in digging a hole for a fence post, straightened his back and wiped sweat from his brow. He screwed his eyes to see better. They were not Indians come galloping down the valley, they were white men.

At first he felt relief. It would be good to talk to strangers and get news of the outside world. Then apprehension gripped him as they drew closer and he saw what a bunch of cut-throats they were. They were yelling and whooping as if drunk. My God! he breathed, and took a run for the house. He could only think of the shotgun he'd left inside the door. He cursed himself for a fool.

He saw Annie and the two younger

children come to stand out on the veranda, curious to see the newcomers. He waved them back.

'Get inside,' he shouted, 'and fort up!' His voice was a panicky shriek.

He looked around for Tim, then remembered he'd gone to round up a horse that had jumped the corral fence. He hoped to God the boy would stay out of sight.

Breathless, he leapt on to the veranda, made a dive inside the door for the shotgun then turned and waited for the newcomers.

They were some way off when his stentorian voice hailed them.

'Hold it, fellers! The first one who rides over that line yonder gets both barrels!'

Mitch Delaney's horse slowed to a trot and then a walk. Delaney's laughter was insolent.

'Spoken like a man, mister. All we want is water and a trade for fresh horses. How about it?'

Steve was suspicious but felt a little

foolish. Maybe they were a posse on the hunt for rustlers. The boss man had a certain authority about him; his speech was educated despite his appearance. But of course any man could look like these if they'd been riding the range for days looking for trouble.

He moved out of the veranda's shadow.

'Who be you lookin' for, mister? We've had no strangers ridin' through.'

'You,' came the brusque reply.

'Me?' Steve was surprised and confused.

Mitch Delaney raised his arm, then brought it down in a signal that was like the slash of a sword. Steve Warton's body was riddled with bullets.

Annie screamed and ran to the door. She looked out, then slammed it shut and, with trembling hands, laid the stout piece of wood across it into its two slots that Steve had carefully made. Then hugging the two frightened children to her, she huddled behind the massive tallboy that housed all her most prized possessions.

Tim had rounded up the maverick horse by tempting it with a carrot and was now riding home, bareback, when he heard the hoofbeats. He was in time to see his father facing the bunch of men with his shotgun raised; then he saw the signal and the fusillade of bullets as his father went down.

He was stunned. He wanted to cry and he wet his pants then reaction set in and he felt hot anger surging through him. He wanted to run amok, firing at the bunch of bastards, but getting killed wouldn't help his mother.

He watched the men break down the door and saw his mother dragged from the house, hair down, screaming and struggling, bodice ripped. He saw little Jess make a break to run towards the hay barn, to be brought down by a big man who carried her back, laughing at her violent struggles to free herself.

Tim looked at the gun his Uncle

Cass had given him. He, on his own, couldn't go to their defence, but what he could do was sneak off and go and find Uncle Cass and the Cheyenne. They would know what to do . . .

3

At the end of a second day's riding, Cass and the Cheyenne entered a long narrow canyon with towering sides, the cliff face hung with various stunted bushes, their roots seeking cracks and moisture to survive. A shallow stream meandered by the trail, dark-shadowed, the water icy cold and crystal clear. The Indians waded upstream, their ponies obviously knowing their way home. Eventually the stream widened, flowing into a steep-sided valley dotted with trees and lush green grass.

As they rode further on, they could now smell horse-sweat and the pungent odour of horse droppings and with it a noxious mixed scent of humans . . . of rotting refuse, wood ash and human excrement. It was a sign of human habitation that Cass had come across many times, both amongst the Indians

36

and the white settlers.

The village, long and straggly, was a mixture of summer tepees and the more permanent lodges of a settled camp. It was a place for the older members of the tribe to settle down while the younger hunters and their womenfolk followed the buffalo.

They saw frolicking children stop and stare and then scuttle away to their mothers but soon there was a crowd of curious Cheyenne waiting patiently to welcome their young chief.

Kingfisher Blue raised an arm in greeting, and an old man with long grey plaits, a brightly coloured blanket about his shoulders, came to stand in the centre of the village. His wrinkled weather-beaten face crinkled in a toothless smile as he lifted both hands in welcome.

Cass watched as Kingfisher Blue slid from his horse on to his feet and faced the old man. He bent his knees and the old one touched him lightly on the shoulder. It was a blessing as between a

37

grandparent and his beloved grandson. Cass looked away, strangely moved by the open affection showing between the two.

Then Kingfisher was gesturing to him to join them. Slowly, Cass got down from his horse, his precious bag under his arm. He felt the piercing stare of the sunken black eyes on him. Cass absently noted the swollen knuckles, the evident pain the old man was suffering from a wry neck and judged him to be far gone with arthritis.

The old man spoke sharply to Kingfisher, who smiled at him and translated for Cass.

'My grandfather has no white man's words. He wants to know if the legend is true and you have magic hands. I told him to remember how you saved my leg but he thinks as you have grown older, then your magic might have waned. He wants to know if you can save Moonstone who is now very weak and has not eaten for the last four days.'

Cass shrugged.

'Tell him I shall know better when I have examined her. I am not God. If it is her time to die, then nothing I can do will save her.'

Kingfisher Blue translated his answer and there came another sharp reply. Kingfisher Blue pursed his lips in disapproval.

'My grandfather says that if you don't save her, you shall accompany her to the hunting lodge in the sky! He is an old man. You must forgive him for his words. He lives much in the past when white men were our natural enemies. He does not understand that all white men are not murdering barbarians!'

Cass looked about him at the men and women crowding close to see him. It was as if he was some strange exhibit.

'Could we cut short this conversation and go and see your wife?'

'Of course.' The young chief made it clear to his grandfather that Magic Hands must see Moonstone forthwith. The old man waved imperiously and

39

nodded, then turned his back on them both. The interview was over.

'My wife is in a birthing tepee with her women. It has been built under the sacred trees and blessed by Black Lynx who is our medicine man as well as her brother. It was built after much ceremony so that nothing should go wrong. I don't understand why all is not well with her. Her women have tried to induce the child, but their efforts have not succeeded. They even built a fire with sacred herbs and the incense from it only distressed her more. We have been in despair.'

'No wonder,' Cass snorted. 'Those women of hers probably nearly choked her!'

They walked the couple of hundred yards away from the village and Cass was pleasantly surprised that the site was clean and clear of the usual everyday rubbish that lay behind most of the lodges.

He paused as Kingfisher Blue raised the tent flap.

'You must understand, Blue, that all those women inside must leave. You will order them out?'

Kingfisher Blue considered with a doubtful look.

'Even her mother? She has the temper of a she-cat when crossed.'

'Especially her. I want no interfering woman protesting at what I might do.'

'What about myself? Can I hold her hand?'

Cass shook his head. Husbands were the most dangerous when wives were in labour and apt to lash out at doctors trying to do what was necessary.

'I'm sorry, Blue. It's me on my own or not at all. I don't want any panicky member of Moonstone's family around. You can see her just as soon as is possible. You can trust me, Blue. You know what I did for you.'

Kingfisher Blue nodded reluctantly, black eyes moist.

'She and I have been sweethearts ever since we first wandered the forest together, even before we knew she was woman and I was man. She is my world, Magic Hands. Save her for me!'

Cass nodded and waited for Kingfisher Blue to bend and enter the tepee. After several minutes, during which Cass could hear shrill protests, the three women inside the tepee came out, glaring at Cass, the eldest screwing up her face and waving her fist at him. So that must be Moonstone's mother!

The young Indian followed them out and ushered the women away, all muttering at him. Then Cass bent and stepped inside. At once the fetid stench of sickness hit him. Without a word he walked across the floor of the tent and plunged his bowie knife into the tough leather buffalo-hide. He made a slit a foot long, then proceeded to cut out a square on three sides so that a flap hung down and a shaft of light glimmered through. He could feel the fresh breeze circulating around the tent.

It was only when he was satisfied that he squatted down and looked at the supine female lying on a bed of bracken covered by a gaudy Indian blanket. Several talismans hung above her head, one of which was the skull of a rat, another was a bunch of eaglet feathers. With them was a huge bunch of sagebrush to keep away the flies.

The girl lying there was in her early twenties. A beautiful girl if one liked the round flat features, but now that round face was gaunt, the eyes were closed and beads of sweat lay on brow and upper lip. Every now and again she groaned and arched her body as pain swept through her.

She opened her eyes as Cass pulled back the upper blanket. She was wearing a coarsely woven cotton shift; between her legs was a pad of cotton-covered lichen and it showed a tell-tale red. The girl was haemorrhaging, or had been.

Her look of alarm and her struggle to sit up ceased weakly as he patted her shoulder.

'Don't be frightened. I'm here to help you. Blue brought me to you.' He wondered if she understood his words. Her relief was evident and so was his.

'Magic Hands,' she whispered, 'you're . . . ' but couldn't say any more.

'Yes, I'm Magic Hands and you can trust me. I am now going to examine you.' She nodded and shut her eyes again as if too tired to bother any more.

The examination was swift. The child was breeched and it was a miracle its heart was still beating. He assessed the situation quickly. She was too exhausted to finish the job herself. It would have to be that which he'd seen done only several times before, but, he thanked God, he'd had a surgeon with vision who'd not only explained the procedure but allowed him to help in such an operation.

He looked about him. This was a hell of a place to tackle an operation of this kind; there was not even an operating table.

He poked his head out of the tepee and beckoned to an anxious Blue.

'How is she?' Blue asked.

'Weak but very brave. Get me a bowl of boiling water, some clean rags and stand guard at the opening. Get ready to receive the baby in due course!'

Blue looked at him unbelieving. 'The baby is still alive?'

'He was when I listened to his heart five minutes ago!' Cass hoped profoundly that the little scrap wouldn't die on him during the operation. God help him if it did!

Kingfisher Blue didn't answer but sped off to hurry the women to stoke up the fire and boil water and find clean cloths. Minutes later he was back, water steaming and with a selection of rags.

Then Cass waved him away and shut the flap so that Blue could not see what was to happen. Then, saying a prayer silently as his surgeon had always exhorted his students to do, he prepared Moonstone for the operation and gave her a whiff of laudanum, just enough to ease the coming pain.

Quickly he sterilized his hands and the steel scalpel in the boiling water, took a deep breath and cut deep into the tight skin of the bulging belly . . .

Outside, Kingfisher Blue waited and so did all the members of the family for Moonstone was a popular girl. Her mother chanted to herself and fingered the amulet bag hanging around her neck, rocking backwards and forwards where she squatted by the fire.

Black Lynx waited too. He was fond of his sister or he might have wished that the white man would fail to save her. If he did save her, then in all fairness the white man was a better medicine man than he was and he must find out his secret formula . . .

Then suddenly they all heard the cry of a newborn baby. A gasp went up. Kingfisher Blue tore back the flap and there was Cass, sweating and grinning and bloodied and holding a tiny scrap of a baby wrapped in a bloodied piece of coarse linen.

'Here you are. You've got a beautiful daughter, Blue. Get those women to wash her and make her comfortable while I see to Moonstone.'

Blue looked at his new daughter. Her eyes were tight shut but one little hand seemed to be searching to grasp something.

'She's beautiful,' he breathed. 'How is Moonstone?'

'Tired but happy. You can see her when I've finished mopping her up. She can't be moved for a few days, Blue. Those women will have to look after her well, but she'll be able to feed the little one straight away.'

'Magic Hands, I'll be always in your debt. I shall not forget.'

Cass put a hand on his shoulder.

'I was glad to help again, Blue. Now off you go and show her to that formidable mother-in-law of yours!'

Cass chose to stay for the next few days to make sure that Moonstone had no complications. Black Lynx and he came to an uneasy understanding; Cass answered many questions and in return Black Lynx showed Cass many herbs and plants that Cass knew nothing about. Cass also found a stream of patients coming to him for all manner of reasons, mainly so that they could say that Magic Hands had treated them and caused miracles to happen. He was to go down in legends that would be embroidered many times in the future.

Ten days after his arrival in the village, an exhausted Tim Warton on a tired and lathered horse was brought in by one of the dog-soldiers who had visited the ranch. He'd been hunting fresh meat when he'd come upon Tim's tracks and had followed them as whoever was riding a lame horse seemed to be going around in circles. Recognizing the white boy, the hunter had brought him in.

Cass was shocked to see him.

Little Fox lifted him gently from his mount and held him upright while Cass went to him.

'Tim, what is it? What's happened?'

Tim opened weary eyes that lit up for a moment and then went dull again as he slumped forward into Cass's arms.

'It's Pa and Ma and the kids! Dad's been shot and God knows what's happened to the others!' Tim began to cry. 'They had no chance . . . '

Cass looked at Blue, who looked blank at the news.

'Have you heard of any uprisings? Are there any Indians on the warpath?'

'It's not Indians, Uncle Cass, it's outlaws. They came ridin' in before dusk, two days ago. I was out lookin' for a horse and I watched 'em surround the house and Pa came out with the shotgun and I tried to run back as fast as I could, Uncle Cass. I didn't even have my gun with me! Then I saw Pa go down, blasted by at least five of the outlaws. They used his body for target practice and laughed while they did it!'

'And your ma and the kids?'

Tim covered his face with his hands and tears trickled through them.

'I heard Ma screamin' in the house and Jess ran outside and a big fella chased her and dragged her back inside. I don't know what happened to

Bobby . . . ' He sobbed while a great anger built up in Cass Warton.

'Are they still there, Tim?' But Tim was sobbing hard now. Cass slapped him lightly on the cheek and the shock silenced him. 'Look at me, Tim. Are they still there?'

Tim nodded, his eyes burning with hatred for the whole world.

'They were when I sneaked away, God damn them!'

Kingfisher, who'd been listening, now moved forward and took Tim from Cass.

'The women will look after the boy. We can be ready to ride with you within the hour.'

Tim pulled himself away.

'I'm comin' with you! I'm not stayin' behind. They're my folks!'

'You can't, Tim. You're all in. You can help the old ones guard the women and children in the village.'

Tim allowed himself to be escorted away and it was Moonstone's mother who finally found him somewhere to

50

sleep after he'd been fed.

The fierce old lady smiled and nodded at Cass.

'I shall look after him as if he was my own. You can trust me.'

Cass left the village with Kingfisher Blue and his dog-soldiers, prepared to take vengeance on the murdering white-eyes.

4

Captain Silas Plumpton, with Sergeant Bill Steel beside him, pulled up and raised his hand; the column behind him surveyed the open country but did not see its beauty, with the surrounding hills in the far distance which looked like a backdrop to some artist's canvas. He was itching from a heat rash and he knew he smelled like the bottom of a pigsty. His arse ached and his stomach rumbled. He scratched the lice in his beard.

'Where in hell are those goddamn scouts? They've been gone two days and we're riding around in circles. I'm sure I've seen that peak before!' He pointed to a distant rock that arose in the air like a giant needle. 'And the water's running out. Surely the bungling fools could find *some* signs of a bunch of horses riding through.'

'It's hard ground, Captain and the varmints will be up to all the tricks to hide their trail,' said the man known to the troops as Sergeant Bill.

'Yeah, but those Apache scouts have eyes like hawks. It's beginning to look as if we've been hoodwinked. That Major Delaney was a tactical expert, you know. One of the best at West Point. He could have made a name for himself if he hadn't indulged his undoubted savagery against his own men as well as the enemy. He's a wily fox, Sergeant. We'll both get the kudos when we bring him in.'

'You think we'll get the chance, sir? I think he'd rather die than be dragged back to Fort Levenworth.'

The captain grunted.

'We'll have to find him first before we find out. But we'll get him, dead or alive. He got away with one hundred and fifty thousand dollars, enough to set him and his men up for life. They won't settle for the easy life of course. That kind don't give up the thrill of violence and easy pickings. They've got to be exterminated like rats, but it's a pity we have to do it! I could do with a decent bed for the night for once.'

He eased himself in the saddle and Sergeant Bill grinned. He was older than the captain by at least ten years and had learned to live and sleep in his saddle, but he remembered what it was like when he was a young greenhorn.

'Mebbee we should rest the horses, sir. No need to kill 'em without cause. They'll have to be fresh if we get within sniffin' distance of the bastards.'

'Yes, you're probably right, Sergeant. We'll take a break now and eat and send a detail out looking for a stream. We need water. Order the cooks to prepare rations for a cold supper. We'll ride on during the night.'

'But sir . . . '

'That's it, Sergeant. The scouts will find us when they're ready to return.'

Sergeant Bill rode down the ranks of men giving out his orders. Soon the camp was being prepared and all the while Bill Steel muttered to himself about the Apache probably not returning because they'd vamoosed or been shot or were just plain idle. The captain relied too much on those two varmints.

★ ★ ★

Cass Warton and Kingfisher Blue and his dog soldiers made good time across the mountains and back along the trail towards the Warton ranch, but it still took the best part of two days.

They drew up in a bunch at the lookout post where young Tim had first spotted Kingfisher Blue watching the ranch. Cass was devastated by what he saw. Far below were the smouldering remains of ranch house and buildings. The corral was empty and several starving piglets could be seen running around in the tall grass looking for their dead mother, her remains still slung over an open dead fire, the body revolving on a spit with each gust of wind.

Cass cursed long and hard and Kingfisher Blue drew near, touching his arm.

'We shall find the men responsible and roast them alive,' he said consolingly. 'Now we go down and perhaps bury the dead.'

But they were surprised to find that only Steve Warton's body was still where it fell, sprawled in front of the ranch house. Already flies buzzed around his eyes and nose as he stared up into the sky.

Cass squatted by him, noting the bullet holes in chest and throat. He counted ten. So the whole bunch must have used him for target practice. He clenched his teeth as tears threatened to blind him. He would get the bastards if it was the last thing he did.

Kingfisher Blue raised him up and led him away, saying softly,

'My braves will prepare a burial site under yonder trees and then you can say your Christian words over him, then we shall eat and follow the trail before it gets cold. Yes?'

Cass nodded. He and his brother had never been truly close because they had chosen different life styles, but as Cass had got older he'd hoped to settle down near Steve, organize a refugee centre and small hospital for the Cheyenne and become part of Steve's family. Now the dream was shattered.

He inspected the smouldering ruins. There, signs of looting and partly burned books lay amongst the ash. A scorched doll and a homemade ball made from rawhide lay half-hidden beneath a pile of domestic items. It looked as if the marauders had been looking for cash and valuables. There were also signs of dried goods being loaded up, for spilled coffee and a half-sack of flour lay amongst the scorched and blackened weeds.

But there was no sign of Annie or the children. It was as if they had never been.

Tommy Eagle Eye, a younger brother of Kingfisher Blue, who was the tribe's

best tracker, loped away, bending low
and searching the ground for signs of
horses moving out. He cut a wide circle
around the homestead, picking out the
strange horses' hoofs from the ranch
horses. He could read sign like a book
and soon he came back and pointed
south.

He raised his hands and showed ten
fingers, then four more, meaning
fourteen horses carrying riders. Then
he counted ten and five again, heavily
laden, and two lame horses.

'Some horses drag hoofs. Ride long
time. Exhausted. They take horses from
ranch. One horse carry wounded man.
He leans to the side and nearside hoofs
dig deep. One horse carry woman and
children and trot with small steps. Very
light. They make for the Devil's Gorge
and the pathway through the mountain,
but not know the way. They go in
wrong direction and then turn at the
gap yonder.'

Kingfisher Blue listened carefully to
his brother's findings and then strode

over to Cass who was kneeling at the foot of a newly built cairn to mark the burial spot.

Cass got to his feet when he saw Kingfisher Blue coming. He jammed his hat on his head, his face grim.

'Well? Did Tommy find any tracks?'

'Yes, more than tracks. He reckons they make for the Devil's Gorge and the pass through the mountains, moving south.'

'So they could be making their way to Mexico. If they reach the Red River, then we might lose them. If Annie and the kids are still alive, they may be aimin' to sell them at the slave markets. We've got to catch up with them, Blue!'

'We'll do that, never fear, Magic Hands. We have fresh horses and know the terrain. We also each have a spare horse so we can ride non-stop all day and all night if necessary. Take heart, Magic Hands. The Great Spirit will help us. We shall get the woman and children back, I promise you.'

'Aye, if they're still alive!'

They ate swiftly, then loaded up. Just as they were ready to leave the valley a lone rider came galloping down the slope towards them. Cass recognized the fair hair of the youngster and swore. Tim had got away from the camp and was now tailing them.

They rode to meet him and though white and drawn, the boy was grimly determined to ride with them.

'They're my folks and I'm entitled to help them,' he shouted when Cass remonstrated with him. 'I've got the gun you gave me and if I'm old enough to use it I'm old enough to fight!' Cass couldn't argue with that.

'Then all I can say is that if you can't keep up, then you can't slow us down and we leave you behind!'

'I'll keep up even if I kill Bonny to do it.' He patted the mare's neck as he did so. Cass grunted.

'Then so be it. Let's get moving!'

Tommy Eagle Eye led the way ahead, Cass and Kingfisher Blue close behind with Tim trailing them and the dog-soldiers fanned out behind them.

It was a silent bunch of riders who followed what Tommy Eagle Eye considered to be an open book. The outlaws were travelling fast but there were signs of tiring horses and they came upon the remains of a thin and gaunt horse that had collapsed and died. Tommy Eagle Eye examined it and reported that the inner body was still slightly warm, which meant that the outlaws were only hours ahead.

At this news, Kingfisher Blue raised his fist and lifting his head high, howled like a wolf as a token of warning to the hunted.

Far away, Mitch Delaney and his men heard the faint cry of a wolf but thought little of it. They struggled to get the tired horses up an incline and into the Devil's Gorge, a long gash in the range of hills which ended after a hundred miles in the pass which brought travellers down again into the foothills ranging south.

Annie clung to her horse, more dead

than alive. In front of her was five-year-old Bobby and behind her, her thin arms clinging tightly to her mother's waist was Jess. Annie had to summon every ounce of her strength, to bear up for the children's sake.

She was still traumatized by the shocking treatment she'd received from Mitch Delaney and several of his men. It had been the little man called Ned who'd saved her from the brutal assault of all of the grinning men.

'No point in killin' the bitch. We could take her with us and we can all take turns, nobody left out. Then when we get to Mexico we could sell her to the Comancheros. She'd bring good money, and the kids too. What d'you think, boss?'

Mitch Delaney had laughed; his own lust satisfied, he was indulgent of his men. It was a good way to keep them satisfied and at the end of it, the captives would fetch at least a thousand dollars.

'Why not? You fellers can arrange a

rota, but mind you, I want first shot at her every night . . . '

And it was so and Annie ached in every muscle of her body. Yet she had to find a way to protect her children.

She heard the wolf's eerie wail and shuddered. She wondered if the nightmare would ever end . . .

5

The riding had been relentlessly hard both for man and beast. The Cheyenne, used to changing horses, rode fearlessly through the night hours instinctively avoiding rough ground and unseen obstacles. Cass marvelled at the skill of Tommy Eagle Eye who never seemed to falter.

Young Tim was grimly hanging on, teeth clenched and every bone in agony. Yet he must be there when the time came to confront the men who'd shot his father. He dared not think of the fate of his ma and Bobby and Jess. To think of them was to unman himself. He mustn't break down.

At last they'd travelled through the pass. Before them was comparatively flat land. Dawn was breaking and gold and pink rays of the sun highlighted the more scattered trees; they could see a winding river in the distance.

'They'll be makin' for the river,' Cass muttered, knowing both men and horses would need water, as they did themselves.

Kingfisher Blue turned his pony towards him and cantered close.

'We wait here. Tommy Eagle Eye scouts ahead. He say many horses lame so white-eyes maybe fort up. They go that way,' his arm swept up and followed the flow of the river.

'You figure there are places to hide?'

'Many places. Caves in rock face. Devil's Gorge always a place of refuge for thousands of years.'

'Huh! So it could be hard winklin' them out?'

Kingfisher smiled pityingly.

'Perhaps for you, a white man, for us, no difficulty! There are secret ways in and ways out of that gorge that only chiefs and shamans know. Black Lynx has gone with Tommy Eagle Eye to lead him in. We shall soon know. In the meantime it will do well to rest.'

Cass took one look at Tim who was leaning forward along his horse's neck, his eyes closed, oblivious to the world around him. Cass lifted him gently from the horse and laid him on the ground and wrapped him in his own blanket. The boy did not stir.

★   ★   ★

Jack Stacy was on lookout. He'd grumbled at the order. Delaney was being too officious. It was like being in the army, goddammit, he muttered to himself. Why the caution? They'd got away and not a sign behind them of the soldiers. He thought of the cash in his saddlebags and cheered up. Life wasn't so bad, especially now they had the woman. The kids were a drag. If he'd been in charge he would have left them back in the scrubland and let the snivelling little swine fend for themselves. But for some reason Delaney had insisted on taking them along. Maybe there was more in it than just selling them to the Comancheros. Maybe the bastard had a soft spot for kids . . .

He lounged, smoking a hand-rolled cigarette and enjoying the sun on his face. One thing, being on lookout meant he wasn't doing any other chores. He took a drag from a hip flask. It went down and hit his stomach with the kick of a mule. It was good stuff, this homemade hooch looted from that old feller, he couldn't remember where. But he toasted the old codger. He was probably making hooch in hell by now. He laughed at the thought. Probably the devil liked a good swig of hooch . . .

His bladder was making him uneasy. He stood up and moved away, unbuttoning himself as he went. He watched his stream scatter some ants on the ground. They were running all ways. Then, buttoning himself up, he cast his eye along the ridge of the far hills and saw the bunched Indians.

He wasn't expecting any humans, neither Indians or soldiers. This was a region of wilderness. He watched them for a while, wishing he'd had Delaney's army glasses. They didn't seem to be doing anything in particular. Probably just a hunting party. He knew there were several Cheyenne villages in these parts, not that he'd ever visited any. Delaney's policy was to keep away from Indians. They had a nasty habit of communicating quickly if any of their members were violated. Best shun the Indians and keep out of trouble was what Delaney believed.

Now, Jack Stacy sat down and took another swig of hooch. He wasn't going to track down to where they were holed up just to report a bunch of measly Indians . . .

*　*　*

Captain Plumpton's troop was making good time. The scouts had returned grinning. They'd ridden cross country towards the Black Hills and the far foothills. He knew the men were fed up

68

to the back teeth at the constant riding. But orders were orders. They had to catch the renegade major and recover the payroll, or he, Captain Plumpton, would find himself humiliated and back in the ranks. Of the two alternatives he would rather kill his men.

'If we go on as we are sir, we'll be well on our way to Mexico . . . *sir*,' Sergeant Bill emphasized the 'sir' as his captain turned and glared at him.

'You heard the scouts' report. We're on the right track. What more can we do?'

'We don't get no nearer, sir. We're just followin' on behind like.'

'What do you suggest then, Sergeant? That we should grow wings?'

The acid tone made Sergeant Bill pull back and ride a safe distance behind his captain. His ears turned red when he heard the sniggers behind him.

They travelled deeper into the range of hills and now all heads were turned to scrutinize the terrain. There were not only renegades to hunt and watch for. There were the Indians, too. Some new recruits imagined Indians behind every bush, despite the assurance of the captain's colonel, that the Cheyenne in these parts were mostly peaceful. 'Mostly' was the important word in this case, the young soldiers thought. It only took one aggressive red man to slam an arrow into someone's ribs! None of the men wanted to be that man.

One scout rode back to the detail and reported.

'Movement ahead, sir. A group of Indians.'

'Jesus H. Christ! That's all we need!' Captain Plumpton was as jumpy as his men. He didn't relish the thought of a skirmish with Indians on the rampage. 'Which way are they heading?'

'Away from us, sir.'

'Thank God! We don't want to start another war with those sons of bitches . . . no offence, Teakettle,' he added, as the Apache scout scowled. The man shrugged.

'They're no friends of mine.' He spat on the ground.

'Right. Then perhaps we should pull in and make camp and let them carry on. It's likely they don't know we're behind them.'

'Oh, they'll know, Captain, no question about that.' Teakettle gave him a look as much as to say *we're not all dumbheads in our own country.*

'You think so?'

'I know so, sir. All red men backtrack and circle, even on a peaceful march with women and children. They know what goes on both behind and in front. I know.'

'So why are they leaving us alone?'

'They're not painted for war. We are not a danger to them. They are out on other business.'

'You mean they're hunting meat?'

Teakettle's face remained inscrutable.

'They hunt meat but not buffalo meat. I think they hunt what we hunt.'

'Why d'you think that?'

'White man rides with them. He

rides with chief.'

'So perhaps they hunt the major. I wonder why.'

The Indian shrugged.

'Much smoke on other side of hills. My brother go that way to find out and maybe follow trail of white-eyes.'

'Hmm! Then perhaps it's just as well we're taking a break. We'll wait until your brother reports back.'

Teakettle looked at him as if he couldn't figure him out. If he had been chief of white soldiers he would have pushed on and joined the Cheyenne party led by the white man and become a stronger fighting force. He lifted his shoulders and strode away. He looked at the sky. The sun was shining overhead. He would go some place quiet and find a boulder on which to sit cross-legged and send up his prayers to the Great Spririt for his brother, Swift Deer's, safe deliverance and the chance to count coup. He wondered if the white men ever prayed, for in Teakettle's view they were barbarians; tales of cruelty to humans and animals had been recounted around the campfires ever since he was a young boy. The only reason he and his brother were scouts for the white man's army was to have a foot in each camp . . .

★   ★   ★

Mitch Delaney surveyed the river, the rocks and the position of the entrance to the hideout. It led to a cave which went far back into the hillside. The sandstone had been worn away countless millions of years ago by water when the river had been wider and deeper. Now the river had shrunk and the dry cave remained. It had a sandy floor and when Ned Scoggins had fashioned a torch by wrapping a bundle of rags around a dead branch and lighting it, they saw that the cave opened out into a sort of cavern, the far end being still unknown because of the gloom.

It would do. It would take so many of the horses as well as themselves. The trouble was, they had a surplus of horses, having taken those from the ranch along with the woman and kids.

Mitch nodded to Ned.

'If we've got to stop, this is as good a place as any,' he said grudgingly. It was against his instincts to stop but the men needed rest as did the horses. They'd lost some horses already. Just up and dropped in their tracks, and the rest looked thin and worn. They had to hole up and rest.

He glanced at the woman still on horseback. He had to admire her spirit, for she was white-faced and gaunt but her back was straight and she clung on to Bobby, while Jess, behind her, held her around the waist, her head leaning on her ma's back. The kid was sound asleep. He nodded to the bunch of spare horses that young Knobby Bowles was in charge of. They were their own original mounts and all were bags of bones.

'Ned, get rid of that lot. They're holdin' us up.'

'But we can't let 'em loose!'

'No. You and Knobby take 'em downriver somewhere quiet and shoot 'em.'

Ned nodded and turned away while the rest of the men unloaded their gear and then led their reluctant horses into the dark interior. With much swearing of men and kicking of animals they were inside.

Mitch swung Bobby roughly down to the ground and turned to help Annie. She refused him, dropped to the ground and turned to help the little girl, now muzzy-eyed and ready to cry.

Mitch's face turned cold at the snub.

'Stop that kid from cryin' or I'll give her somethin' to cry about,' he said sharply, then, taking hold of Bobby's wrist, he dragged him inside the cave, knowing that Annie would follow. She was rarely more than a few feet from either child.

She had fought like a wildcat when any of the men tried to take either child away from her: they had the scratches and bites to prove it.

But she gave herself quietly to whoever wanted her. She would close her eyes and detach herself from what was going on. Her own honour had been violated so many times. It did not matter any more. It was a kind of payment for leaving her children alone and the men had come to respect that.

Now she huddled down with Bobby and Jess on her sleeping bag and watched while the men prepared for the night. A fire was built Indian fashion inside a pile of stones, so that the flames did not betray them to unseen eyes. Dry wood was used which gave off little smoke and that was grey rather than the billowing black smoke of green wood.

She and the men heard the shots that came in quick succession. There was a pause; then Mitch said laconically,

'OK, fellers, just Ned and Knobby doin' what was necessary.'

They went on with their chores. Soon, coffee was brewing and thick lumps of bacon were being fried and some of Annie's looted preserves was being opened, peaches in syrup went well with bacon . . .

Ned and Knobby returned. A job well done and the carcasses were far enough away not to smell upwind . . .

High in the sky above a lone buzzard circled, unseen by Ned or Knobby. Then by some mysterious means, several more congregated and danced the dance of death above the still-warm bodies. They would circle there until the stink of rot rose high, then they would swoop down and tear at the flesh . . .

⋆ ⋆ ⋆

Tommy Eagle Eye, travelling fast and watching the trail before him paused to wipe his brow. It was hot in the undergrowth and he was having to lead his horse while he sought out the tell-tale signs of many riders passing by. It was easy to be distracted by other trails but now he'd got a good fix of horseshoe patterns in his mind. He could nearly go ahead blindfold.

He looked around him, an invariable habit, then looked upwards. He saw the circling buzzards far ahead. It looked as though something were newly dead. The birds weren't ready to pounce yet. That meant the kill was too fresh for their palates.

He turned from the path he was following. He would investigate and see what animal it was that had died there along by the river . . .

The sun was casting long shadows when he finally came to the hollow by the river and saw the horses. There was one for each finger and two over. He waited. But nothing stirred except for the quiet slow movement of wings as the buzzards waited patiently.

He left his horse tethered under a shady tree and then ran, crouching as he went for fear of a trap. Nothing stirred so he circled the hollow, looking at the skeletal condition of the animals.

The buzzards wouldn't find much meat on them, he thought as he examined them in detail. Then he lifted a hind leg of one and felt its belly. It was faintly warm. Just as he thought. They were newly killed, so that meant he was closing in on his quarry.

Now he rode carefully, watching for the first sign of men coming to this hollow. He followed the sign upstream; when he got a whiff of smoke and coffee he dismounted and left his pony far enough away from the smell of strange horses and moved in close. He wanted to observe how many men there were and if there was any sign of the woman and kids.

He darted from tree to tree, using everything for cover. Now he stepped carefully, not breaking a twig or frightening any birds that might be roosting close by.

Then he saw the lookout man sitting on a boulder out in the river. An easy target: he was tempted, but it would betray his presence. No, he had to watch and observe and then go and report to his chief.

Then, his eyes now adjusted to the twilight, he saw that the majority of men were housed in a cave. He smiled to himself. Of course! He had heard the legends of the Cave of the Skull, reputed to be in these parts. Perhaps this was the place and if it was, then there were other ways to enter the famous sacred cave. He had heard Black Lynx talk many times about the miracles wrought in the Cave of the Skull. He would know how to enter . . .

6

The cave was beginning to smell. The long line of horses, tethered to a strung-out lariat along one wall, were restive, uneasy about their surroundings. Their manure and urine gave off steam and Jack Stacy grumbled. This idea of lying up in a cave wasn't so good after all.

He took a firebrand and moved further into the cave, the dark recesses being as yet unexplored. He was surprised at what he saw, for the walls of the cave were painted with designs of crudely drawn beasts: buffalo, deer, mountain cats and smaller animals like jack rabbits and coyotes. But what made him draw in his breath was the huge grinning skull. It dominated the cavern and it seemed as if the sun behind it was sending down light rays right through it.

He realized the paintings were ancient. Some of the paint was faded, while some colours were as bright as if painted only yesterday. There were human figures too. Warriors with bows and arrows and spears firing at huge shaggy buffalo; there were also men with animal heads.

Suddenly his skin crawled. He didn't like what he was thinking. He peered into the gloom, no longer wanting to explore to the very end of the cave. He wanted to be back amongst his fellows.

Ghosts!

Shamefaced, he looked around, imagining ghostly fingers touching him. The old-time medicine men used magic. He'd been told that over and over again when he was a kid. He knew all about spells and such. He hurried back to the dim light of the fire and so missed the two openings, hidden far back in the hillside, and the tunnels beyond.

Mitch Delaney looked up sharply as Jack came stumbling back, his expression somewhat wild. Mitch frowned.

'What in hell's happened to you?'

'I don't like this place. It smells evil. There's paintin's back there . . . '

'It's hoss shit and piss. We'll be out of here just as soon as the hosses rest up.'

'It's not the hosses. It's them there paintin's. This cave was a sacred place. God knows, those red bastards might have made human sacrifices here!'

'So what? The place hasn't been visited for years, not even by animals, so quit bellyachin'.'

'That proves it, doesn't it? If animals steer clear then there's somethin' wrong. I say we should get out before somethin' horrible happens.'

'Are you goin' loco? We need those hosses fit. We've a long ride ahead if we mean to get into Mexico! Goddammit, Jack, you're free to move out with your gear any time you like.'

They glared at each other and the other men drew close, eagerly waiting for the outcome. None of them felt any loyalty either to Delaney or Jack Stacy. It was every man for himself, but staying along of Mitch meant excitement and loot without having to figure out raids for themselves.

Now they watched for Jack's reaction. If he left, he would leave with what he had in his saddlebags and nothing else. He'd also lose the use of the woman and his share in what they made from the sale of the woman and kids to the Comancheros.

Jack backed down and turned away.

'I'm only tellin' you this place has an evil smell to it. I'm not thinkin' of quittin'.'

'Good. Now do somethin' useful and go outside, clear your head of cobwebs and keep watch . . . and keep your eyes peeled. You might miss a ghost otherwise!'

The men laughed uproariously at the joke and Jack felt humiliated, his anger spilling over as he cautiously made his way outside. He found a cluster of rocks high up behind which he could sit comfortably while he watched the river in both directions. One of these days,

he would show that bastard what was
what . . .

★   ★   ★

Kingfisher Blue listened to Tommy
Eagle Eye and for once his face twisted
into a grin. He put a hand on his
shoulder.

'Well done, Eagle Eye. Now we know
where they are, we can use white-eye
strategy and rescue the woman and the
children before we begin the assault.'

He turned to the listening Cass and
translated for his benefit. 'The men are
holed up in the Cave of the Skull. Eagle
Eye has not seen the woman or the
children but expects them to be
prisoners inside.'

'But how can we get to them?'

'There are ways, my friend. Those
barbarians think they have found the
ideal hideaway, not realizing it is still in
use.' He laughed and it sounded strange
coming from him. 'We do not leave
clues about our presence in the ancient

medicine grounds. We do not leave traces of our spirits to pollute the atmosphere and so we leave everything as nature intended.'

'So what do we do?'

'Wait. We shall hold a powwow with the Great Spirit and he will tell us what to do.'

'But that is time lost!'

Kingfisher shook his head.

'Time is not lost. Time is as nothing. The moon rises full tonight. We shall invoke the gods of the winds and rain and of thunder and lightning and place our problem with them. You shall see, one or more of the gods will aid us.' He nodded confidently. 'Yes, you will see for yourself.'

So Cass waited, worried and impatient and doubting. He would never understand these red men if he lived with them for the rest of his life. He talked to Black Lynx to pass the hours away and learned many secrets of the red man's medicine. He also imparted the white man's knowledge of medicine to an interested Black Lynx and found they had many ideas in common.

They ate around a small campfire and Cass noticed an air of tension building slowly. The young braves were keen and eager for action, all hoping to count coup once again.

The moon rose, dark clouds scudding by and the campfire died down to a glow amongst the deep layer of embers. A smell of incense filled the air and mingled with the woodsmoke.

Cass, sitting cross-legged beside Kingfisher and Black Lynx, was aware of a stir around him.

Then came the drumbeat, steady and regular. Cass blinked as the braves came and squatted in a circle around the embers of the fire. The drumbeat came faster and the men swayed to its beat.

Then an ululating sound came from the forest behind them as if some animal out there was being summoned to the ceremony.

Cass found himself holding his

breath. This was the stuff of dreams. He, a realist, was seeing something uncanny happening that he would never be able to explain logically. He rubbed his eyes for surely he must be dreaming. All around him was the incense, and the scent of it growing stronger. Vaguely he wondered whether someone had sprinkled some substance on the glowing embers of the fire.

Then he saw the golden glow amidst the faint grey wisps of smoke rising gently into the night sky from the nearly extinct fire. The light wavered and then shot upwards as if to connect with the full moon above.

Then, startled, Cass watched as lightning flashed and tore at the ball of light and a sinewy figure, naked except for a black lynx-pelt draped over head and back, whirled into the golden light and started to dance.

Cass glanced to his side and saw that Black Lynx was gone. Now he knew why he was so named. He had within him now the soul of the lynx.

A second and a third drum began the beat that Cass soon realized was in keeping with a human heartbeat. As Black Lynx's gyrations grew faster so did the drumbeats; it was as if all those who crouched in a circle connected to the drumbeats with their own hearts.

Then everyone was ululating and Cass found he too was joining in. It seemed right and proper to do so.

A great wind sprang up from nowhere and rushed by, branches of trees shaking and ending in a swirling vortex, disappearing upwards towards the moon. Then came dead silence as both wind and lightning disappeared.

The surrounding terrain and everything alive within its boundaries appeared to be listening. A faint growling in the distance faded away, as though some animal had gone back to its lair.

Then the rains came.

★   ★   ★

Jack Stacy got to his feet and clambered further up the hillside so that he could see better. Something was going on out there. The Indians were making a rare old racket and it made him uneasy. Not that he was worried for their own sake. The Indians weren't hunting them, only the soldiers. But all the same, he wondered what mischief the redskins were up to.

He saw the lightning flash, heard the sudden rush of wind, and relaxed. The goddam heathens were probably trying to avert a thunderstorm. It was amazing how these primitive people knew when bad weather was coming, he ruminated.

When the rains came he cursed. Bloody rainmakers, that's what they were! He might have known. He ducked under cover, wishing he was inside the cave; uncomfortable, maybe, but dry.

★   ★   ★

The rains obliterated the fire with a hissing of steam and the circle of men broke up. Cass was bewildered. Was that it? The golden light was gone and so was the whirling figure. He blinked. God! Had he dreamt all he'd seen?

Then Kingfisher Blue was tugging at his arm.

'We must go. We have much to do.'

'What? Why? What's happening?'

Kingfisher Blue smiled slowly.

'The spirits have spoken. The rains have come and we must act fast.'

'But why?'

Kingfisher Blue shook his head as if at a stupid child.

'The rains. When they come as they are coming now, there will be a flash flood and all surface water will make for the river. The tunnels leading to the Cave of the Skull will run with water. You understand?'

Cass looked at him, horrified.

'You mean, after a few hours the water will fill that cave?'

'Not fill it, run through it and

91

everything will be washed into the river, which will rise and break its banks.'

'Then we must get Annie and the children out.'

'Now you understand why we must move fast!'

7

Teakettle squatted cross-legged on a flat boulder and faced the east. He was waiting for sunrise so that his prayers would rise directly to the Great Spirit himself and cut out the lesser gods.

He had done this many times during his service with the white-eyes. He looked down on those same men and considered them barbarians. They knew nothing about the natural world and killed for the sake of killing. They polluted the earth, leaving a trail of disaster and were oblivious to the power of the Great Spirit. They even poisoned the waters, a heinous crime in Teakettle's eyes. But the fact remained that he needed the support of the military. It meant he knew their plans. They were useful too, in that they waged war on the Cheyenne enemies, which was good.

Even now, Swift Deer was reporting back, via smoke signals to watchers to the south, of the troop's movements, and he himself was covering up for Swift Deer's absence.

None of the troop, even the most experienced, had the wit or understanding to question the faint plumes of smoke that rose at intervals above the mountain ranges.

Teakettle viewed the white-eyes with contempt. They were like babes left alone in the desert to die. They didn't even guess that Teakettle was leading them around in a giant circle to mark time while he was checking on what the Cheyenne were doing, riding out with a white man heading the group.

It was natural curiosity on his part. The Cheyenne had always been the natural enemies of the Apache in days gone by.

Now he was waiting for that vision that would come to him, as it had done before when he had needed advice from the Great Spirit himself.

He chewed leisurely on the juicy cactus leaf . . .

The vision came just as the first strong rays of the sun came over the horizon in a star-shaped burst. He closed his eyes against the glare which threatened to blind him. He heard the deep drumlike voice erupt all around him, making his ears vibrate. He felt sick. He fell back, conscious of the cold flat stone digging into his back. Then he knew no more.

The sun was high when Teakettle opened his eyes. Swift Deer was squatting over him, slapping his face. He looked grim.

'Wake up, brother! You have spent too much time communing with the Great One. The captain is angry that you stay away so long!'

Teakettle looked around him and then sat up sharply.

'Ha . . . aa . . . ee! It is good you have come. My spirit has been flying over the mountains. I have seen many things!'

'Come now, brother, surely it is the

juice of the cactus talking?'

Teakettle shook his head.

'Not so. It was the will of the Great Spirit himself. I visited the sacred cave and there was much sorrow and evil there. It is being polluted which is against the Great Spirit's wish.'

'But the sacred cave is guarded by the Cheyenne. It is their responsibility surely?'

Teakettle smiled and shook his head at his younger brother.

'The Great Spirit does not recognize differences within tribes. We are as one when we defend the Earth Mother from the barbarians. We must go help the Cheyenne!'

Swift Deer pulled a face.

'Do they really need help? How do we really know they are near the sacred cave?'

'Are you an unbeliever? Do you not recognize a direct command from the Great Spirit himself?'

'But brother, I did not have the vision. You did!'

'You call me a liar?' Teakettle leapt to his feet and twisted round to face Swift Deer with knees bent and one hand already feeling for his knife.

Swift Deer looked alarmed and stepped back, hands outstretched to calm Teakettle's sudden anger.

'You mistake me, brother. You are no liar. I merely said I had not the vision. I believe you.'

'Then why the doubting questions?'

Swift Deer shrugged.

'Perhaps because I was jealous. I have never had a vision.'

'And you never will if you harbour the worm of doubt in your head,' answered Teakettle caustically. 'In the meantime we must report back to the easygoing captain who wants the mad-dog major to fall into his hands without much effort!'

'Can you blame him when his troop is made up of braves who have not counted coup?'

Teakettle nodded.

'It is the old man, the sergeant I feel

sorry for. He has the responsibility of the troop and knows the danger. I respect him but not the captain. If it wasn't for our arrangement with the tribe, I should be gone moons ago!'

'We must not break faith with the tribe, that would be suicide. They depend on us to keep them informed as to the army's deployment. Where would they be if we did not intercept the messengers from the Army Command?'

They both laughed. It was so easy to waylay the messengers, fill them up with rotgut whiskey, get them to boast about their superiority over the Indians. Teakettle and Swift Deer would smile and take any insults and then put a white man's dollar down between them and bet they couldn't read the white man's words on the papers the messenger was carrying.

It always worked, and, in the morning, they remembered nothing about it and weren't even aware they'd been robbed of their silver dollar . . .

Now, they both raised arms to the

rising sun and turned in the direction of the troop's temporary camp.

It was time for action, and Captain Plumpton and his men were going to find out what a forced march was all about.

★ ★ ★

Mitch Delaney walked down the line of horses tethered on a lariat in the depths of the gloomy cave. He carried a makeshift torch and examined each animal. He was concerned with what he saw. Saddlesores and swollen tendons predominated. The horses were thin and their rib bones showed. Two had lost shoes and were limping badly, with swollen hocks. They would have to be taken out and shot, for any food was wasted on them.

He inspected the sacks of oats. Very low. Soon they would be existing on dried grass only and God knows that was sparse in this goddamn country!

He wanted to move on but judging

by the state of the horses they'd have to wait another day at least. They were dead if they didn't have horseflesh. No one but goddamn Indians survived out in the arid hot land with its scarcity of water away from the river itself.

He was having niggling doubts about this enterprise. Everything had gone wrong that could go wrong, and the men were uneasy and grumbling even though they had the woman to take their minds off their gruelling ride to reach Mexico and safety.

He heard the distant growl of thunder. The air was stifling hot and humid. No wonder the men's tempers were frayed. He was jumpy himself and this goddamn cave had an atmosphere about it that was giving him night-mares.

He barely glanced at Annie and the children. Why in hell he'd brought the kids along he couldn't fathom. Maybe it was to make sure the woman did as she was told quietly. She certainly hadn't caused a fuss when he first took her. He smiled to himself. Could be she liked it. Other women had enjoyed his sexual prowess. Why shouldn't she?

But even Annie's meekness had come to bore him. He no longer looked at her with desire. It wasn't much fun with a woman who lay quietly like a soft down pillow while he strained and sweated.

Still, she was useful for the boys and kept them in line even if they did grumble about conditions.

He squatted down by the fire. Ned watched him over the flames, not liking Delaney's grim look.

'So? What d'you think? Can we make it to Mexico with them there hosses?'

Delaney spat into the fire.

'Like hell! We'll have to seek out other horses. It means another raid and that gives anyone following us a first class lead as to where we are.'

'Maybe we've shaken off anyone following us!'

'Are you crazy? The army never give up! They'll be out there somewhere with some goddamn eagle-eyed scout

101

trotting after our tracks. Remember, I know how they work. A bottle of whiskey for the scout who sniffs us out and a buck for every goddamn one of us who's killed and a couple of gold eagles for the redskin who brings me in! I don't want that, do you?'

Ned Scoggins stared at him.

'You really think they're still on our trail?'

'Haven't I just said so? This is no time for bogeyman jokes. That's why it's essential we leave as soon as possible.'

'You should never have ordered the raid on the military train! That was a mistake!'

Delaney shrugged.

'None of you thought that when we shared out the cash. You're free to go, Ned, any time. But I warn you one man on his own has little chance of getting to Mexico!'

'You son of a bitch! We haven't much choice have we? We either stand or fall together.'

'Now you're seeing sense and you can talk to those ungrateful bastards out there. Grousing isn't going to get us to Mexico. Remember that!'

Ned's eyes smouldered. He was losing confidence in Delaney fast. He'd thought it a smart move to go along with his major in the beginning. The smooth-tongued slime-ball had made it all sound so easy. Knock off a bank or two, rob a couple of mail trains, burn out a ranch and move on in no time at all, each man would have a tidy bankroll and then they could all go their own way and live it up for the rest of their lives. It would be wine, women and song all along the line.

The reality was bleeding flies and sweat and sore arses, mangey food, dung beetles, one half-dead woman to share between them all, and little to drink. Life was hell.

Ned reached for the coffee pot. Even that was watered down until it had hardly any kick. He poured a tin mugful and drank.

'When I get to Mexico City I'm going to have me the best rooms in town and as much real coffee as I can drink, the best woman in town and a dozen bottles of the best whiskey to go at!'

Delaney's face crinkled in amusement.

'When, Ned, when! I like a man with a goal in mind!' He turned his back on Ned and hunched down, putting his hat over his eyes. He might as well rest while he had the chance.

★　★　★

Captain Plumpton sat inside his tent with the flaps open. The air was still and heavy and he was sweating even though the sun had gone down. He eased his high uniform collar. His neck seemed to have swollen with the heat and his collar rubbed, making a tiny red sore on his skin.

'Goddamn it!' he bellowed and his batman, Toby Pelham, rushed into the tent, a washcloth in his hand. He was just cleaning the captain's boots for the morning. He prided himself in keeping the captain looking his usual spick and span self even if he did have to rough it in this cursed land.

Toby Pelham had been the captain's batman since young Silas had graduated from West Point five years ago. This was their first real trek into the wilderness, and Toby wasn't very happy. He saw Indians behind every bush and every creaky branch meant an arrow was on its way to some unlucky target. Toby was as jumpy as a frog in the mating season.

'Sir!' He stood to attention before the captain.

'For Chris'sake! Relax. We're not on parade now, Pelham. It's these god-damn mosquitoes. I've been stung on the neck again. Bring me some of that coal oil. You said the smell might keep the little varmints away.'

'We haven't much left for the lamp, sir. It's the light that attracts them, sir.

If you would sit in the dark at night . . . '

'What? Sit in the dark? Not on your life! A feller must have some creature comforts. How in hell would I see to pour me another tot out of the demijohn if I didn't have light?'

Toby Pelham was tempted to tell him that he could drink out of the jar neck like the hill-billies did, but thought better of it. He couldn't see one of the finest products of West Point drinking out of a mug let alone straight from the jar.

Captain Plumpton had brought six fine crystal glasses with him in his baggage. Up to now only one had been smashed, and that was because one of the baggage handlers had been clumsy.

He was glad it wasn't himself who had done it. He'd never heard such vulgar language come from such well-born lips and wondered where the high and mighty captain had heard it in the first place.

Toby regarded his captain's temper

with pride. He respected him for it. There was more to Captain Plumpton than met the eye.

'Go on, Pelham, bring me some in a tin if you can find one in this goddamn camp.'

'Yessir!' Off he went to find something to hold the small drop of stinking oil. He slopped some and cursed. What he'd lost would mean the oil would run out for the lamp that little bit sooner.

He brought a couple of spoonfuls in a tin salvaged from the camp's rubbish dump. It had contained peaches. The tin itself was lead-lined. Pelham doubted it would be a healthy thing to do, to rub coal oil on to a mosquito bite, but it was the captain's neck not his.

He watched while the captain opened his collar and shirt and rubbed his neck, wrinkling his nose against the smell.

'Sir, you'll have to be careful when you light up a cigar . . . '

'Yeah yeah yeah! I'm not a fool,

Pelham.' He sounded drunk and Toby gave him a wary eye, gauging just how much he'd drunk and how soon would he have to tuck him into the fancy cot he'd brought with him.

'Sir, should I wipe away the surplus?'
'Nah . . . leave it. It'll soak into my coat collar and kill the damned fleas! Why in hell I ever thought it the gentlemanly thing to do, to join the army, I'll never know.' For a moment there was silence and Toby did some clearing up, noting a couple of dirty glasses and an empty champagne bottle. The captain had certainly been pushing things tonight. God knows what would happen if the redskins decided to attack!

Then Captain Plumpton nodded his head.

'Yes, I remember now. It was a girl. Can't remember her name but she liked uniforms. Thought they made a man look tough and handsome. She was the first girl to flirt with me. She twirled her fan exquisitely and her eyes promised much. I joined up to impress her. My ma cried but my pa was proud of me.' Again he brooded. Then he said softly, 'She never did let me kiss her, only hold her hand. She laughed when she saw me in my new uniform, and you know, I never saw her again.' He looked about him. 'If it wasn't for her I'd not be here in this stinking hellhole now!'

Toby Pelham listened quietly, the stink from the coal oil nearly choking him. He'd have the devil's own job getting rid of the smell and stain tomorrow and most likely he'd get a tongue-lashing for the state of the captain's uniform jacket. The drunken bastard would never believe he was himself to blame for that mess. It was a dog's life being a batman.

Far away in the distance the thunder rolled around the hills and faint flashes of lightning lit up the night sky. Toby watched it for a while after he'd tucked his captain up in the cot in the army tent. To Toby, the storm seemed to be coming closer. Ah well, let it come, he thought as he pulled off his own boots ready to settle down within earshot of his officer. Sometime during the night that one-quart bladder would have to empty and Toby kept a china chamber-pot handy. Captain Plumpton didn't believe in going into the bushes to relieve himself when he had a batman to do the dirty work for him.

Toby pulled the grey army blanket about his own head. He pitied the guards on duty. At least he didn't have guard duties to do. He was a bit above that. He closed his eyes and soon was snoring. He never heard the heavy patter of rain. Only his master's voice would rouse him . . .

★　★　★

Swift Deer looked at Teakettle with awe. The Great Spirit had responded to Teakettle's supplication in record time. It had only been that morning that Teakettle had had his vision. The Great Spirit must think highly of his brother. He wished he too could be so holy. It would mean so much more prestige in his tribe when finally they went home. From being the white-eyes' scouts to holy visionaries would be a great step up indeed and two brothers was better than only one member of the family being exalted. But how did one become proficient in visions?

Teakettle laughed when he asked the question. They were both crouched high in a tree watching the river rise. They were on the opposite bank of the place of the sacred caves.

They were cold and wet and there was nothing to see. Yet both knew that inside the caves was a crowd of wanted men and their horses.

Swift Deer envied them. They were warm and dry even if they were defiling a sacred Indian site. Swift Deer's belly rumbled. It was a long time since he'd eaten and he could have done with some of that fire-water the white-eyes loved so much.

'How much longer should we stay here, brother?'

'Just long enough to make sure that we've found our man,' Teakettle answered grimly. 'We would be as nothing if we brought the troops here and these men were not those we hunt. Do you want to be laughed at?'

Swift Deer had not thought of this possibility. It went against his vision of himself as a man who knew everything. He shook his head, the drips of water cascading down below on to ground that was being churned into mud. He cursed, for the drops were icy cold.

Teakettle put a hand out to warn him. There was movement up on the rocks opposite. There was a guard and he was awake. They watched while the man urinated from above, Swift Deer admiring his flow. The man who could send out such a powerful stream must be well endowed. To kill a man of his prowess would enhance that man's sexual strength, just as killing a mountain cat would give a man all his strength and attributes.

Swift Deer made a move. He was going to snake down the tree, find a suitable place and send his arrow across the river to slam into the man's heart.

Teakettle put a hand out and stopped him.

'Wait! What do you think you're going to do?'

'Kill him and take his strength. I will become a great lover!'

'Don't be a fool! Do you keep your brains between your legs? If you kill him now, then the troop will never catch them. Remember we want the major. You and I can share the gold for finding him. Think of the whiskey we can buy! You can take all the girls you need without that man's strength! Leave him be.'

Swift Deer was disappointed.

'I wanted to see whether it would happen to me.'

'And if it did, you have no woman here to prove anything! Be smart and wait. There may be another chance to send him to his own stinking hunting ground.'

Swift Deer nodded.

'True. You are very wise, brother. So what do we do now, apart from dying of cold?'

'We go back and report and if that captain who has no guts thinks the time has come to do battle, then perhaps you might have your wish, little brother!'

They moved like shadows down from the tree and moved away, hugging the darkness. The guard who was still watching from above was oblivious to their passing. He stretched and paced up and down for a while, then went back to his shelter to rest.

8

The rain came cascading down in a steady stream, bouncing off leaves and hitting the ground with an ominous plop and a rhythmic sound like music. Cass watched, fascinated. Surely that ceremony hadn't really invoked this storm?

He looked at Black Lynx with added respect. Something had happened but his reasoning wouldn't accept what he saw. Yet the result was very real.

'What can we do now?' he asked. 'How much time have we got?'

Kingfisher Blue shrugged, his face inscrutable.

'We must cause a diversion. We must lure them out of the cave; as for time, only the Great Spirit knows that.'

'But you must have some indication?'

'The ground is hard. It will take time for the subterranean channels to fill. It

115

depends on how much rain falls and how long it lasts. But be assured, the underground rivers will flow, and when they do, they will find a way to the river. That way is through the sacred caves. You understand?'

Cass nodded. It was logical. He knew about strata of rock and water tables and these people living close to nature knew exactly what would happen. It was part of their religion.

'So how do we go about getting them out in the open, seeing as it's raining so hard?'

'Free the horses! It won't take much to stampede them when the thunder rolls and echoes in those caves. They'll have to go for the horses. They mean life or death to them.'

'And?'

'We attack! They'll not expect an ambush!'

'Mmm, it might work. What if they leave half their men behind to guard the caves?'

'We'll attack them from inside. There

are other ways into the caves as well as from the river.'

Cass looked at the young chief with admiration.

'You've got it all worked out, haven't you?'

'As much as possible. But things could go wrong. The important thing is getting the woman and children away from there.'

'And if you lose some of your braves doing it?'

'Then that is their reason for being on earth and they will have fulfilled their destiny. They will be rewarded in our spiritual home.'

'But . . . '

'No more talk! My mind is made up. It was destined when you found me as a youth, half dead. You brought me back to life. This is my way of repaying you and for what you have done for Moonstone.'

Cass lowered his head. There was nothing more to say.

More wood was flung on the fire. It

sizzled, the flames leapt up and danced and Cass saw Black Lynx throw some powder into the heart of the flames. They turned blue.

Then the braves sat facing Kingfisher Blue and Black Lynx, and Cass sat back and closed his eyes as the men debated on the right strategy to use.

He roused himself when the circle of cross-legged figures sprang to their feet and leapt into the air, each with one hand upraised. The battle cry ululated from their lips.

They were ready to go. To Cass's gaze they seemed to have changed into savage hunters . . .

They waited for dawn. In the meanwhile they ate a frugal meal and drank the potent Indian brew. In the background a drum beat softly, its effect keeping courage high and fear away.

The man on guard outside the cave shivered as he heard the eerie sound. He was cold and though he huddled under the shelter of a boulder he was damp and his fingers were numb.

From time to time he drank whiskey but though it hit his stomach with blistering heat, it did not reach his extremities. He wished his relief would come so that he could put some hot coffee down his throat and huddle under his blanket. He thought of the woman, soft and warm, but knew he would not be one of the lucky sons of a gun who would enjoy her tonight.

He listened to the drum and wondered where the pesky Indians were and what they had in mind. He wasn't afraid. There was no indication that they were aware of the white-eyes being in their vicinity. He reckoned they were a passing hunting-party, probably getting drunk and boasting of their prowess at hunting, and this strange habit of counting coup. Funny bastards, Indians and their uncouth ways. More like animals . . . He yawned. He could have slept if it hadn't been for that damned drum which seemed to echo in his ears.

Then Jack Stacy was poking him on the shoulder.

'Some guard you are, Nick Fallon! If I'd been a huntin' red son of a bitch, I could have knifed you and you wouldn't have known a thing about it!' He kicked Nick in the ribs.

Nick opened his eyes wide. He'd slept and didn't know it! It must have been the hypnotic beat of the drum . . .

'Hell, Jack, I must have just dropped off. That drumbeat got on my nerves.'

'That stopped an hour ago, you pesky sidewinder! Wait till I tell the boss!'

'For Chrissake don't do that! You know what a filthy temper he has!'

'Look, feller, a guard that sleeps betrays his buddies. Those fellers rely on a good guard so that they can relax and sleep. You must know that, Nick.'

'I didn't do it deliberate,' protested Nick. 'I sure didn't. It must have been that drum!'

Jack sighed and shook his head.

'Not the drum, Nick, it was the whiskey! How many times has the boss said no drinking when on guard?'

'Christ, Jack, have a heart. It was rainin' frogs and toads, remember? A feller needs somethin' in his guts.'

'Well, mebbee I'll forget it this time, Nick. You owe me.'

'Much obliged, Jack, I'll not forget.'

'I'll see to that,' Jack replied ominously. Then he raised his head sharply. 'What in hell's that?' From below there came much screaming and yelling and from the cave mouth there issued a cloud of blue smoke.

Then as Jack and Nick stared at the sight with surprise, they saw several men stagger outside, choking and coughing. Behind them were a mass of struggling horses, obviously panicking. They streamed out of the cave and, turning, galloped off along the river bank, and spreading out as they went.

'What in hell happened in there?' The two men started to clamber down from their vantage point towards the cluster of men.

Mitch Delaney, without his boots on,

was bawling orders. Ned Scoggins was trying to hold back the stragglers with some of the men.

Mitch Delaney saw Jack and Nick.

'Don't stand there like fools! Go and help round up those goddamn horses!'

'What? How in hell do we do that on foot?'

'Use your head, man! Ned's managed to keep some back. You and Ned and some of the boys can go after them, for Chris'sake!'

Jack nodded at Nick.

'You do it. I've got to help the boss look after this end of things.'

'Why me instead of you?' Nick grumbled.

'Because you owe me, that's why!'

Nick shrugged and made off towards the spooked horses that Ned and the boys had prevented from escaping.

He looked at them sourly. They were the slowest and boniest of the whole sorry string. Not good enough for cat's meat, but they were their only hope of rounding up the others.

Ned looked at him.

'There's seven. You can have your pick.'

Reluctantly Nick saddled up and rode out with Ned and the other reluctant volunteers. Mitch Delaney watched them go, then turned his attention to that strange blue cloud which had devastated everybody. Then he went to inspect the lariat rope holding the horses in line.

Just as he suspected, the line had been cut.

What in hell was going on?

His first reaction was to go and see the woman and the kids. Maybe they had got loose and she'd cut the rope, but then that didn't explain the strange blue gas, or was that from the bowels of the earth and the rains had somehow displaced the gas from some under-ground cave? He had heard of such phenomena before, especially in places where the earth seeped a kind of oil . . .

But Annie was still fastened by the ankle, the two kids huddled beside her, frightened and bewildered.

Mitch reckoned he knew what had happened and gave Annie a cursory glance, his mind on the cave itself. It put the shivers up him. He could feel its menace. He'd be glad when they were well away from the cursed place.

Now they would lose valuable time while the roundup went on. The horses wouldn't gallop far. They were in no condition to do so, but it didn't augur well for them for they needed all their meagre strength to get them all to Mexico.

Mitch Delaney cursed his bad luck. There sure were demons putting the big X on all his plans. He wondered whether he should pack his bags pick the best two horses and make off during the night and to hell with everyone. But that meant leaving the woman and she was worth real money down in Mexico as well as providing him with her body on the way.

Christ! It was a dilemma. He fingered his bristly chin. He'd have to make his mind up before nightfall.

Now the long wait was on. He hoped those lazy sons of bitches would get a move on and get that herd right back. When they did so, those fellers would want to know his plans for moving on.

Whether he stayed or sloped off, he would have to have a plan ready. The boys were shrewd. He couldn't risk them thinking he didn't know what to do next. He had to be ready for them.

★　★　★

Cass and Kingfisher Blue crouched low behind huge boulders. They watched the horses come plunging out of the cave, gallop along the river bank and fan out over the fast-puddling ground as the rain came down.

Water dripped from Cass's Stetson but he was hardly aware of it. He marvelled at how Blue's plan was working. The faint drifting blue gas that issued from the cave was a sight that he didn't understand. He turned to the

125

crouching Indian beside him.

'That gas, how did you work that?'

Blue grinned.

'That's part of Black Lynx's magic. You white medicine men don't know everything. We have secrets that have been passed down for generations.'

'But how . . . ?'

Blue shrugged. 'Black Lynx knows these things. He studies the workings of the natural world, listens to Mother Nature herself. He knows that when the great rains come, strange things happen underground. Gasses are formed deep down in the earth and they have to find a way out. That gas we see is released from deep fissures in the rock far below ground.'

'So you knew from the beginning that anyone caught in those caves at a time of the rains could be doomed?'

'Yes. For those ignorant and unaware, they could be trapped for ever.'

'Then there is good reason to get Annie and the kids out fast! Not only because of the excess water rushing through the caves but because of danger from the gas?'

'Yes. You see how the horses panicked. But have no fear. Those horses didn't get loose on their own. I guess Black Lynx will even now be leading them out.'

Cass looked on Kingfisher Blue with admiration mixed with fear. He hoped Blue was correct in thinking Black Lynx was even now leading Annie and the children through those twisting tunnels, but if he was wrong . . . He felt sick and helpless. He could do nothing to help, only wait and watch.

Then after, it seemed, an eternity, he heard gunshots and the cracking of whips and yells as the bunch of horses were herded back to the cave mouth.

He felt his innards tighten with tension. This was what Kingfisher Blue had been waiting for. He glanced sideways at him and saw the Indian's usually impassive face drawn in grotesque anticipation, with lips stretched showing sharp teeth, likening him to some ferocious animal ready to strike.

For the first time, Cass saw him as the white men's enemy, a force to be reckoned with. It was only Blue's obligation to him that made them friends. After the obligation was honoured, what then?

Suddenly Kingfisher Blue's arm was raised, and the heart freezing battle-cry of the Cheyenne filled the air. It swelled and echoed around the hills as the Cheyenne took up the cry, then the sharp unmistakable sound of a gun exploding was the signal for the panic which ensued.

Jack Stacy, high on the lookout point, heard the battle-cry and raised himself up to look around. He couldn't believe what he was hearing. There had been no indication of Indians stalking them. He heard the report of the gun: looking down he saw the horses milling about in front of the cave entrance and most of the men out in the open.

He saw a man fall from his horse and being trampled. Jesus! What was happening down there? He grabbed up his rifle but he could see no target. Panic was beginning to hit him. It slowed his brain. It was like ghosts taking potshots at the men. Now those same men were letting blaze with rifles at any puff of smoke, coming from the undergrowth across the river.

Suddenly he saw movement from the top branch of a tree. The bastards were like monkeys. He willed himself to be calm and cool and stood exposed while he levelled his weapon and fired two shots.

He saw the distant body catapult out of the tree. But his satisfaction was short-lived. As he reloaded, he took a shot in the throat. He never knew what hit him, nor was he aware of his body plunging down like a rag doll to hit the rocks below.

Mitch Delaney cursed. They were like rats in a trap. There was a growing pile of bodies, both men and horses, rising in front of the cave entrance. He rallied the remaining men and they used the growing pile as a barricade.

He still could not believe how quick the onslaught had been. How easily they had been trapped.

He sweated. A slight graze on his cheek from a splinter of rock oozed blood. The air at the front of the cave was now thickening from the noxious gas that was seeping from the subterranean channels and the growing stench of cordite as bullets hummed like angry bees.

He emptied and loaded up as fast as he could and his rifle grew hot. He cursed when it seized up; he threw it away and grabbed up a rifle lying by a dead body. Young Chas wouldn't need it any more . . .

Mitch Delaney was suddenly overwhelmed with superstition. Was this the day his luck was running out? His fingers trembled as he aimed and fired into the thickening fog of smoke. It was like fighting ghosts . . . He tried to shrug the feeling away. It must be because of these damned caves and the eerie atmosphere . . . It had been a mistake to camp out in this place.

He also noticed that the trickle of water running from the cave was now more like a stream and that the walls of the inner cave were dripping. The noise the drips made seemed to grow louder.

He snapped off another shot as Big Aldo slumped down beside him, a spreading stain from a shot in the head.

★   ★   ★

On a distant peak, Teakettle and Swift Deer knelt and watched the panicked horses come bursting out of the cave entrance and spread out along the river bank. Teakettle frowned. Something had spooked them from within.

They watched the men spew from the cave and the panic as some of the men tried to catch the few remaining horses.

Then Teakettle, holding his army glasses to his eyes, gave a grunt of satisfaction. He saw the man they were hunting come at a run from the cave and wave his arms angrily while obviously giving orders for the mounted men to round up the strays.

Teakettle drew a deep breath and then smiled at Swift Deer.

'We were right. The ex-major is chief. We can go back and report to the captain.'

Swift Deer nodded and gestured for the glasses. He too saw and confirmed the sighting.

Both scouts were angry and resentful at Captain Plumpton's reaction when they'd returned earlier and reported a band of white men holed up in the sacred caves and being stalked by the Cheyenne.

Teakettle had made his report to Sergeant Bill. They had waited with arms folded while the old sergeant had passed on the news to Captain Plumpton, who'd been in the middle of his dinner and had not wanted to be interrupted.

Sergeant Bill had waited for his

captain's reaction. He was ready to call his men to arms and be ready for the orders to move out. But Captain Plumpton had other ideas.

He was suffering from the army cook's slovenly cooking and the restricted army rations weren't doing his guts any good. He suspected he had the makings of an ulcer. He burped and looked up at Sergeant Bill.

'Look, Sergeant, do you take me for a fool? I'm not going hell for leather up into them there hills on two scouts' say-so that Delaney might, just might be running that outfit! I want proof that the bastard is there, before I put myself, you and the rest of the men through a gruelling ride that might be just another useless false alarm!'

'But sir, the chances are good that Delaney is their boss! How many other outfits are running loose in these hills?'

'I'm not going into statistics, Sergeant. Just forget it!'

'So what do I tell the scouts?'

Teakettle's and Swift Deer's faces

remained inscrutable, but inside both men were seething. They strained to listen to the captain's words. He didn't even lower his voice.

'Tell the lazy bastards to do the job they're paid for, properly. They never should have come back without confirmation that Delaney is with that crowd. See that they're fed and send them back again. I don't want to see their red hides again until they can bring news of Delaney. I'm not about to make war on any outfit. All I want is Delaney and then we're going home as fast as these jaded horses will take us! So get moving, Sergeant!'

'Yessir!'

The sergeant had relayed the orders in as tactful way as possible. He saw the gleam in the scouts' eyes. God help Plumpton if ever those scouts turned nasty. He wouldn't like to be in his shoes . . .

So now the scouts were ready to ride back and report and if the idle, misbegotten son of a white bitch put on his spurs and found the guts to ride, they could take the man Delaney with no trouble at all; that is, if the captain wasn't frightened off by the news that the Cheyenne were also gunning for the outfit.

Briefly Teakettle wondered why the Cheyenne were attacking the white men so savagely. Probably some trouble over the white men raping their women . . .

They were back in camp within hours. At first the captain was suspicious.

'You're sure those bastards saw Delaney?'

'Yes sir. They described him and Teakettle had my field glasses. Both men saw him. He was organizing the round-up of the horses which had got loose. They also saw him when the Cheyenne attacked . . . '

'Attacked? Jesus! You didn't say anything about the Cheyenne being on the prod!'

The sergeant watched the colour drain from his captain's cheeks. The yellow-bellied son of a bitch was just about shitting himself, thought Bill Steel contemptuously. How in hell he ever got a command like this he would never know. He should have been a pen-pusher in some out of the way Washington office. Probably wouldn't even have been able to organize army rations, never mind writing out orders.

'Sir, as far as we know, there are no organized uprisings by the Cheyenne. This could be a small group fighting a private vendetta, as it were.'

'That's only your surmise, Sergeant.'

'Sir, I've had twenty years' experience and we've had no warnings from any of the forts. The Cheyenne skirmish amongst themselves. If we fall in now, we would be there ready to help them out. It could turn out to be a good relations project.'

'Don't be a fool, Sergeant! They'd cut us down before we could powwow with them and voice our intentions!'

The sergeant shrugged.

'We have a treaty with the Cheyenne

at the moment . . . '

'Which means nothing if they've whipped up a killing frenzy! No, we'll wait and let the Cheyenne flush those bastards out and then we'll go in and mop up. Save the men and the hassle. Tell the men to be ready at the crack of dawn.'

'But sir . . . '

'That's an order, Sergeant!' The captain glared at the older man and then hacked at the last of his beef steak. 'Tell the cook this steak was as tough as leather and if he's not careful I'll reduce him to the ranks. There must be someone around here who can cook!'

The sergeant did not answer but saluted, turned smartly and left the tent.

Outside the two scouts waited, expecting to get at least a pat on the back for the welcome news that Delaney was found . . .

9

The climb up the rocks had been incredibly hard and Tim Warton would never have believed it possible for an old man, as Tim reckoned Black Lynx to be, to outpace him in the way he had if he hadn't seen it for himself.

The youth, Twisted Foot, who walked with a limp and was about his own age, was nearly as agile as his mentor, Black Lynx. Tim felt shame that he was the one who puffed and gasped and that when they reached the crevice of rock which would lead down into the tunnels, they had time to rest and wait for him.

Black Lynx surveyed him with humour in his black eyes.

'The nephew of Magic Hands is not used to climbing cliffs. It takes a lifetime to learn to climb, so feel no shame white boy. Have you slept with a woman?'

Tim blinked and flushed. What kind of a question was that? He would never have discussed that kind of thing with his own father. Emotion welled up in him again as he thought of him and he fought back tears. Hell! These Redskins would think him a softy if there was even a hint of tears.

'Well? Have you been with a woman?'

'Why do you want to know?' Anger chased away his earlier emotions.

'Because to go down into these tunnels you must be pure and a blood-brother. This entrance is secret to the Cheyenne. You must become Cheyenne and then you will honour our traditions and never reveal the secrets you will learn later.'

They stared at each other and Tim licked his lips, wondering what becoming a blood brother entailed. He thrust out his chin. Whatever it took, he would do it, to help save his mother and his brother and sister.

'I've never been with a woman, indeed I don't know any girls and I'll do whatever you want and regard it as an honour to become a member of the Cheyenne.'

'Good. Spoken like a true brave. Your uncle will be proud of you. Come!' Black Lynx beckoned him into the great black hole while Twisted Foot stood by, grinning and waiting to follow him in.

Tim found natural hand- and foot-holds in the rock face and followed Black Lynx down into a blackness he'd never experienced before. He found himself using his other faculties, like touch and hearing, and a latent instinct to feel for and find his way down.

He could hear Twisted Foot breathing heavily as he followed behind but only a movement of air betrayed Black Lynx's passage into that suffocating blackness.

Then Black Lynx was lighting a torch already placed for such an emergency. He was using a tinderbox and the familiar scrape of flint on tinder was a comforting sound. Tim's feet felt for and found the rough rocky ground; he stood back and recovered his breath and realized he was all tensed up. His muscles ached.

Then Twisted Foot was beside him and, as the light grew stronger, he saw the tunnel twisting away into the darkness. The roof dipped so that they had to bend low to protect their heads. The ground was strewn with loose stones which made walking difficult.

The narrow passage, gouged out of rock by water thousands of years ago, now dripped with the water that seeped through the upper rock. They seemed to be walking for an age before the tunnel widened into a small cavern.

Tim's eyes widened when he saw what it contained. Surely those rows of ivory-white balls, neatly stacked, weren't skulls? He moved closer as Black Lynx turned slowly around, holding the torch high above his head.

He was evidently looking for something.

Tim shivered. He'd never seen either a skull or a whole skeleton before. His imagination was playing havoc with him. He wanted to get out of this dread place and climb up that shaft and breathe fresh air. He felt a wave of hysteria nearly overcome him.

Then he felt Black Lynx's hand on his shoulder.

'Think of your mother and the children,' he commanded quietly and Tim was conscious of a calm come over him.

He took some deep breaths and stood still, waiting.

He watched as Twisted Foot found a cache of torches. As each one was lit it was placed in a roughly wrought sconce on the wall of the cave.

Then Black Lynx turned to him. Now he was solemn, his eyes half shut. There was an air of something strange about him, as if he was partly in a trance.

Then, taking Tim's arm, he led him to a corner of the cave. Tim saw that there were bright but crude paintings on the natural rock face and, on a huge boulder, there sat a shallow bowl shaped from a solid piece of black graphite. There were dark stains on it like bloodstains after a pig was killed, thought Tim in sudden fear.

Black Lynx raised his arms and began to chant while Twisted Foot knelt on the ground and howled like a wolf.

Tim watched and listened, fascinated. It was like living in a nightmare. Then Black Lynx scooped up some of the sticky blood from the shallow bowl and turned to beckon to Tim to come closer. His black eyes were opaque and seemed to be seeing things beyond Tim's shoulder. Then he was speaking in a sing-song voice as if repeating words he heard at a distance. Tim stared at the hand coming nearer, sticky with brownish-black blood.

'This is the blood of countless generations of Cheyenne. In it is the essence of many souls and all Cheyenne past and present are represented in this holy liquid which represents all life. The first cave dwellers helped to create this sacred cave with the Great Spirit's guidance. He sent down the Spirit of the Water who loosened the rock and so made it possible for the First People to begin the task of creating this sacred cave. They and the later Cheyenne mark their passing by the skulls which record their time on earth.'

He paused as he drew the sacred signs on Tim's face with the treacle-like substance on his fingers. It seemed to burn into Tim's flesh.

'By these signs I bring you into the circle of the Cheyenne and now you are one of us. Give me your hand.'

Tim, bemused and still a little frightened and overawed by the flaring torch, Black Lynx's ritual and his trance-like state, held his hand out stiffly before him, and then watched as Black Lynx drew his knife from his belt and sliced a small deep cut in Tim's wrist. Then he did the same to his own wrist and as the blood flowed, he pressed his and Tim's wrists together. Tim watched as the mingled blood from the wounds dripped into the dish until it pooled bright red on top of the congealed black blood underneath.

'Now your blood mingles with mine and we offer it to the good of the Cheyenne people who will follow us in the future.'

Black Lynx seemed to listen as Tim held his breath, his eyes riveted on the steady drip of blood into the bowl. He felt strange, as if he suddenly belonged; he no longer felt afraid of this place or of being underground. It was like being on familiar ground. He drew a deep breath and all at once he felt free and he knew instinctively that their mission would be a success, that he would see his mother again and hug his brother and sister.

Then Black Lynx spoke for the last time in this place.

'There, it is done. You are Cheyenne

and the Great Spirit sends his blessing. What has happened to your family was destined to bring you here at this time. You were born for greatness, Tim Warton. Your future is plain for those who can read it. I, Black Lynx, am privileged to see a little and I can tell you now that your path lies with your uncle, the great Magic Hands. You too will know the satisfaction of following in his footsteps.'

'But he's a doctor, I'm only the son of a farmer and farming is all I know.'

Black Lynx smiled and put both hands on Tim's shoulders, one hand leaving a bloody mark.

'You will see I speak truth. You will tread many paths in your lifetime, but the main one will be in Magic Hands' path. You will see. Now, we go and we find your mother. She needs our help.'

Then after bending knee and head in the direction of the skulls, Black Lynx moved to leave the cave and continue his way down the exit tunnel. Tim and Twisted Foot followed.

Twisted Foot had watched the ceremony quietly. His respect and awe of the white boy was now very marked. He, used to Black Lynx's trances and predictions, was impressed. He was an apprentice medicine man but it would take years before he was recognized in his tribe as an experienced shaman. This boy known as Tim was something special. He must look after him and protect him. He now knew why he'd been chosen to come on this expedition.

The tunnel dipped so that sometimes the men crouched as they moved along. Then the ground would rise and the walls widen into small caves, or smaller tunnels would lead away from the main one. Black Lynx seemed to know which tunnel to choose when they came to a fork. And all the while the walls dripped with water until gradually they were splashing through it ankle deep and their feet became numb with the intense cold.

As the torch flared from draughts of

fresh air issuing from deep cracks in the upper strata of rock, they could see ancient paintings crudely drawn. At first the scenes depicted the sun from early morning, as if it had just given birth, to the full noonday sun and then the gradual going down until the death of the sun enclosed by night. Then there were the crude drawings of animals newly born, their life and their death. There were pictures of young trees, their growth, the budding of leaves and flowers and fruit and then the gradual dying of the tree itself.

There were many illustrations going through the cycle of birth, life and death until Tim realized, with some of the better later drawings, that the cycle of birth, life and death was the whole theme and meaning of these caves.

Those long-ago First Cave People and the Cheyenne who followed knew the secret of life. It was something Tim had never thought about. Suddenly he wanted to know more.

He caught up with Black Lynx when

the tunnel widened.

'Tell me more, Black Lynx. Tell me more about the People and the caves.'

Black Lynx looked at him and smiled.

'So the Great Spirit is working inside you already, Tim Warton. You feel the holiness of this place, so now you know that evil must not be done here and if it is . . . ' he paused for a dramatic moment, 'then the person responsible for the defilement will face a life in limbo in the next world. What a man or woman sows, that he or she must reap.'

'That man, Delaney . . . ' Tim swallowed a lump in his throat, ' . . . if he has violated my mother . . . '

Black Lynx nodded.

'He most surely will suffer. A bullet would be too kind. He must suffer for all the evil he has done on earth, not just what he may have done to your mother. He must pay before he is allowed to move on from limbo into the next life. You know about such things?'

'No. I know we are born and live out

our alloted time. My pa read to us from the Bible, but he didn't believe in ghosts and such and he reckoned once we were dead, that was it. We were just carrion like all the animals.'

'Even animals have souls. We only kill animals for food and anything else we need from them to sustain our lives but we always say a prayer and ask forgiveness for taking the life of that animal and thank it for sacrificing itself for us.'

'You think they know?'

'Oh, yes, they know and we feel better when we eat that animal and use its pelt. They give themselves to us as a gift and we thank them for it and bless them. We never kill for pleasure like white men do, like the way the buffalo have been slaughtered for pelts and the flesh left to rot on the ground for the birds and buzzards to feed on and set up a stench on the plains which reaches right up to where the Great Spirit resides. For if we did that, the Great Spirit would become angry and send

150

the plagues of death like the white men's smallpox and fevers and then both animals and men would die in their thousands. No, Tim, we live by the laws of nature and these caves remind us of what is the right balance of life and death. We are reminded at all times that we have just so much time here on earth and we must live according to the natural law. You understand?'

Tim nodded.

'I never thought of life as being a taking and receiving. I wonder if my pa ever thought that way?'

'Possibly he did. He farmed his land and improved it. He grew crops and bred his animals and he gave back sweat and hard work as well as fertilizing his land. He did it by instinct. Your uncle lives by the same token. He gives his time and his love and his expertise, whether for a white man or a red man. I doubt Magic Hands would ever refuse anyone who needed help. It is not in his nature. At first I doubted him. I was suspicious. I thought no white man could know what we medicine men know, but I was wrong. He taught me much and I was privileged to teach him many things about nature that he did not know. We could work well together.'

Tim smiled at him. Suddenly he was no longer in awe of him. He wanted to say that he should like nothing better than to learn from him and become like him.

The words hovered on his mouth but now Black Lynx's attention was upon the faint light ahead. He put up a warning hand to both boys to stand and wait, then he crept forward to see what was happening past a bend in the passage. Then he was waving his arm and they joined him to watch the scene in front of them.

Tim stared, astounded that such a large high-ceilinged cavern could be possible underground. He had no previous knowledge that such places existed.

There were flaring torches at the far

end and he could see movement in the gloom. So the cave was occupied. He could smell horses and the rich scent of manure and knew that they had come upon the hideaway of the outlaw gang.

But where amongst all these men and horses was his mother and the children? His heart beat fast. They would soon be reunited and the thought made him want to cry.

But it wasn't that easy. Black Lynx pulled them back along the passage.

'Patience,' he hissed. 'We must wait until the right time.'

'And when will that be?' whispered Tim.

'When the Great Spirit sends a sign.'

'But how . . .'

Black Lynx's hand came across his mouth as a stumbling figure started to walk towards them. The man had no torch and, staggering and giggling a little, selected a spot, pulled down his trousers and squatted. There were some loud noises and the man started to hum. After a few minutes he stood up and, sighing with relief, pulled up his pants and buckled his belt and stumbled his way back to the group by the cave entrance.

'Dirty bastard!' Black Lynx muttered. 'He defiles the sacred cave! There will be a judgment on him!'

'But *how*?' Tim asked desperately.

Black Lynx looked around him and up at the ceiling and waved an arm about him.

'Look around. Don't you see? The rainwater is gathering fast. Already it runs like a stream and is gathering at every beat of Mother Earth!'

'Then what happens?'

'The tunnels will fill and the water will run with a vengeance that no man can withstand. It has happened many times before and it will again.'

'You mean these tunnels will flood?'

'Of course. Have I not said so?'

'But what of my folks?'

Black Lynx smiled. 'We shall get them out. Never fear!'

Tim trembled with anticipation. His

imagination was running away with him. He was overwrought and visions of another flood like that in the Bible his father used to quote so much, swept over him. It could be the end of the world!

'How do we find my mother?' he gasped.

'You boys stay here and watch. I am going to free the horses. They should not suffer because of the evil the white men bring with them. Stay calm.' With that, Black Lynx crept away silently, like a breath of wind.

Twisted Foot put a hand on Tim's arm and pressed him to squat on the damp ground.

'Relax, Tim Warton. I am here to protect you. If you squat, you may meditate yet still keep the senses alert.'

'I can't do that. I don't know how.'

'Then I shall teach you. It will take your mind off the waiting. Now close your eyes and clear your mind . . . '

Tim did as he was told. He was conscious of thoughts jumping about like frogs, but Twisted Foot's whispered words soothed him and soon he rested and time slipped by as they both waited.

Black Lynx moved lightly on the balls of his feet, his senses stretched like those of his namesake. His eyes appeared to glow bright in the darkness. He was bringing to his aid all the tricks his old shaman taught him many years ago.

He heard the growl of thunder and knew that the Great Spirit was warning him to be ready. He smelled horsedung and was affronted that the sacred cave was being contaminated. The Great Spirit would surely cleanse this place.

He saw the row of horses loom up in the gloom as he moved like a shadow. There was no one at the back of the cave. It appeared that all the men were clustered at the cave entrance as if they were uneasy about being in such surroundings.

He heard the curses of the men as

the rain came down in a raging torrent. Already the drips from the cave's ceiling were heavier, and coming down from the tunnel was a stream that carried sandy silt. The horses were now getting uneasy. Some were straining at the holding rawhide rope and snorting while others kicked out against the rising water.

Black Lynx had seen no sign of Annie and the children. He reckoned they must be tied up on the other side, well away from the horses. The first job was to free the horses, then he would locate the woman and send Tim to free her. If he, Black Lynx, loomed up beside her, she might scream and wreck their plans. No, Tim had to free his mother.

He ran at a crouch along the horses, a hand on each rump humming the same tuneless sound that helped to tame their own ponies. It worked and each horse he passed stood quietly, head moving up and down and ears twitching as if waiting for further orders.

Black Lynx smiled to himself. All horses responded when you tuned into them. He'd learned that when he was a boy.

Now he pulled out his knife and slashed the rope holding them together. As it loosed and parted the horses reared and their own head-bridles slipped free. Black Lynx slapped one on the rump and jumped back as it sprang forward and made for the cave entrance, with the rest following behind.

He heard the shouts of the men, some of whom were watching the river rise, as they dodged out of the way of the galloping horses.

There were screams and yells and Black Lynx smiled at the pandemonium. His part of the job was done. He listened hard. He thought he heard gunshots but was not sure whether it was thunder.

He turned and ran swiftly back to Tim and Twisted Foot. They would now have to find the white woman and her children. That might take some doing as the cave was large and the torches were now nearly all extinguished because of the water pouring down. They could also be hidden in a small cave. It would be a painstaking search unless someone came to free them before they drowned . . .

Tim jumped when Black Lynx silently joined them. He opened his eyes. Surely he hadn't slept? No, he was sure he'd been aware of his surroundings and yet . . . He looked at Twisted Foot who was laughing at him.

'What happened?' he asked.

'You are a good student, Tim Warton. You were suspended in time.'

Black Lynx looked sharply from Tim to Twisted Foot.

'You haven't been playing your tricks on Tim? This is not the time or place to experiment with your meditations! Come, we must now find Tim's mother!'

They scrambled to their feet, Twisted Foot looking pained.

'I was but helping Tim to have patience while you were away. It saved him a lot of worry. See, he is rested and not a bundle of nerves!'

Black Lynx grunted. He would have to take that little know-all in hand when all this was over. If anyone should teach Tim Warton about the Cheyenne way of life it should be he, Black Lynx, not some jumped-up precocious young upstart, just because he had the ability. He would have to learn a lesson the hard way and know that he had to creep before he ran.

He put a hand on Tim's shoulder.

'Use your instincts. See with your inner eye. We must not use light or we might betray ourselves to those who may be watching. We must move slowly and sense our way and if possible, unite with your mother's aura and she will guide us.'

'I can't do that. I don't know how!' Tim shivered in the dark.

'Forget your own fears. Put her need above your own. That way your senses will begin to work. Have no fear. This is a lesson for you. I shall find her and you will greet her for she will trust you, where she may be frightened and scream at the sight of me. You understand?'

Tim nodded. Already his fear was subsiding as he thought of his mother. He ached to hold her and the children in his arms.

It took time to creep slowly down the cave and explore each aperture and small cave. They split up and Tim accompanied Black Lynx while Twisted Foot moved slowly along the other side.

Tim was conscious of conflicting sounds and smells. The water flowing around their ankles was rising. If they did not get out soon, they would be trapped.

Then Black Lynx suddenly stood still, putting a warning hand out to Tim, for someone was coming at a blundering trot with a spitting torch that flared and sizzled as drops of water fell on it.

It was Mitch Delaney, He was cursing as he made his way to a small opening and looked inside. He stayed only a moment, then returned to the cave entrance. Black Lynx whispered softly to Tim.

'That is where your mother is. Now you can go and bring her back here. Take my knife and hurry!'

Tim stumbled away, one hand running along the rough rock until he came to an opening. He heard breathing and was aware of movement in the darkness.

'Ma?' Then he heard the exclamation of surprise.

'Tim? Is that you, Tim?' There was a sob in her voice.

'Yes, Ma, it's me, Tim. Where are you? I can't see you.'

'I can see you standing in the opening, a dark blob against a faint greyness. We're just a few steps away from you, Tim. We're all together but we're tied by the ankles.'

'I've got a knife, Ma. Keep talking

and put out a hand and grab me when I come near.'

He moved forward slowly, then he felt her hand clasp his wrist. Then he was kneeling down beside her and her arms were about him and he was conscious of Jess and Bobby straining to get near him and touch him.

It was quite a business cutting them free in the darkness but at last it was done and Tim warned the children to be quiet and not be afraid. He led them back by touch until he had rejoined Black Lynx and Twisted Foot.

Annie was trembling, she moved like an old woman, and it was a shock to see the two Indians with Tim, but Black Lynx soon reassured her.

'I am Black Lynx and this young brave is Twisted Foot. You gave us your hospitality, Mrs Warton, ma'am, when Kingfisher Blue came seeking Magic Hands. You remember?'

Tim, who was holding her upright, felt her relax.

'You remember, Ma. You baked bread

and we used that side of bacon we were saving for winter.'

Annie nodded slowly.

'It all seems a dream now and long ago. Where are you taking us?' Her hands instinctively went out to encircle Jess and Bobby.

'We must move quickly. We go back through a tunnel leading to the surface far back from the canyon itself. Those white men know nothing about these outlets that the Cheyenne have been using for hundreds of years. But now we must make haste for the Great Spirit grows more angry as time goes by.'

He put out a hand and touched her. 'Have no fear. Soon, we shall come to the place where we left our torch and the way will become easier. Tim will look after Jess and Twisted Foot will see that Bobby comes to no harm. Now we must make haste. You will keep one hand on my belt and if you stumble I shall be there for you. You understand all this?'

'Yes, and thank you, Black Lynx. I

never thought we should ever leave that cursed place!'

'Not a cursed place, Mrs Warton. Only the men who took you there are cursed. But their punishment will surely come from the Great Spirit himself.'

They moved ahead, Black Lynx leading the way with Annie beside him, then Tim and Jess followed closely by Twisted Foot and Bobby.

After a short time, Jess kept stumbling and Tim lifted her up on to his back. She clung to him as if she would never let him go again. It was hard going, for now the stream of water was running fast and they were wading up to their calves. Tim's legs ached and became numb. He gritted his teeth and saw that Twisted Foot showed no sign of distress. If he, with a crippled foot, could grope his way through the tunnel in such horrific conditions, so could he, Tim.

Tim moved his legs like an automaton. He was aware of Bobby sinking down and Twisted Foot scooping him up, throwing him over one shoulder and striding on. The winding tunnel seemed to go on for ever. Were they still in the same passage or had Black Lynx lost his way? He knew the passage widened and they'd struggled through caves but to Tim they all appeared the same.

Then suddenly they were in the cave of the skulls. Black Lynx held his spitting torch high and there they were: the rows and rows of white skulls that shone like polished ivory. Tim felt a great relief. This was the place where he had become a member of the Cheyenne.

He found himself sobbing. He couldn't help himself, and he couldn't care less what Black Lynx or Twisted Foot thought of such unmanly behaviour. All he wanted was to get his family out of this place and to see the blue sky and breathe in the fresh air. Oh, how he wanted it! He would never grumble at the weather again. He would even dance in a downpour of rain or roll in the snow or welcome a roasting from a summer's sun, just as long as he was free. He never wanted to be in the darkness of hell again.

The rope ladder was still waiting. There was water puddling in the bottom, and with it had come topsoil which was now glutinous and coating the sides of the entrance like sticky treacle.

Black Lynx swung himself up the rope and shouted that all was well; then he fashioned a sling and soon, with Tim's and Twisted Foot's help, Annie and the children were hauled up and out of the chasm. They stood blinking and shivering in the rain until Tim let out a great whoop of joy, then they all clung together in a kind of thanksgiving, while Black Lynx and Twisted Foot stood stoically by, impatient at the delay.

They had to find Kingfisher Blue and Magic Hands to report that their mission was successful.

In the distance, muffled by the unceasing rain, came the report of gunfire. Black Lynx cocked his ears to listen.

Somewhere, the Cheyenne were engaged in what they did best. Black Lynx sniffed the air like a bloodhound.

Then he tapped Tim on the shoulder. 'We must go. There is much to do. We shall escort you all back to our camp and then we must find Kingfisher Blue and help him do the Great Spirit's work! Vengeance will be sweet!'

10

Captain Plumpton raised an arm to halt the detail. He and the sergeant surveyed the approach to the river. He glanced at the two Indian scouts riding one on each side of the column.

'Is this the place?' he called to Teakettle, who edged his horse nearer to the captain.

Teakettle nodded. He was in a surly mood. He and his brother, Swift Deer, had worked hard and long for this arrogant spineless son of a bitch and had got little thanks for it. He made a sweep of his arm.

'River overflow its banks. Make treacherous riding. Two, three hours' riding to reach sacred cave where white men hide out. We wait and they come down the river.'

'What d'you mean, they come down the river?' Captain Plumpton's tone was sharp and derisory as if Teakettle was a fool. 'How can they come down the river? Why should they?'

Teakettle sighed and glanced at the old sergeant meaningfully. He shook his head slowly.

'You not understand. The great rains wash out caves. Men will be washed away!'

'But they will have warning. They can climb up the cliffs and out of reach of the water!'

'Not so. They will have no warning. Those who might escape will find cliffs too slippy for footholds. They are trapped.'

'So we sit and wait?'

Teakettle shrugged.

'The Cheyenne also wait.'

Captain Plumpton looked uncertainly at the sergeant and then at the men waiting behind him, all protected from the rain by waterproof slickers covering themselves, their rifles and their horses' rumps. Still they looked a bedraggled lot.

'I think we should take advantage of the Cheyenne being about their business. We don't want to horn in on them and give the wrong impression. No need to risk our men . . . ' His voice trailed away and he coughed to hide a certain embarrassment.

Teakettle hid a smile. He knew the captain would find an excuse not to take part in any skirmish. At least it would give the men time to rest and he and Swift Deer needed to relax and tend to their horses. But he cursed to himself when the captain turned to him.

'Perhaps you would take a look and see what they're up to while the men make temporary camp and eat. Teakettle, get your rations from the cook and arrange with your brother to send smoke signals at intervals. That way the sergeant and I can keep up with events. Right?'

Teakettle nodded. He nudged his horse and rode down the lines to the chuckwagon in the rear after waving at

Swift Deer, who joined him.

'So the cunning snake wants information but will do nothing about it,' Swift Deer greeted Teakettle grimly.

'Yes, you heard him? Watch out for the smoke from yonder peak that sticks up like a finger. A thin smoke means all is well, a wet woodsmoke means the Cheyenne need help.'

Swift Deer nodded.

'I'll be watching.'

Teakettle ate quickly, then stowed away extra jerky and bread. After filling his canteen and drawing extra ammunition from the army stores he was on his way. He was oblivious to the rain which was now turning to a drizzle. The ground steamed and soon he was picking his way along the river bank. He could hear distant gunfire.

He gauged the flow of the river as it churned its way through the gorge in white-water fashion. No one would live in that turbulence if he was unfortunate enough to plunge into it.

He came to the place where he and

Swift Deer had waited and watched. He saw that a battle was in progress. Horses milled about at the mouth of the cave and he knew that the Cheyenne were hiding amongst the trees and behind boulders and were taking their time in picking the white men off like rats in a barn.

Then as he crouched, intent on what he was looking at, the cold prick of a knife at the back of his neck sent a warning through him. He froze, not daring to move. He flexed his muscles ready to spring up and face his assailant if the opportunity arose. But the pressure of the knife increased as a hoarse voice said softly,

'What is a lone Apache doing in these parts? What is your name?'

'I am known by the big chiefs in the army as Teakettle and I am a scout. The Apache are not at war with the Cheyenne so you can take the knife away.'

'Not until I know your business here.'

'My chief is hunting for the man

173

known as Mitch Delaney, ex-major and outlaw.'

'So all you want is Mitch Delaney?'

'Yes. Captain Plumpton has orders to take him back dead or alive.'

The knife was removed and Teakettle risked a look at his captor, noting the angle at which he wore his twin feathers. A Cheyenne of some importance, well muscled, who no doubt had claimed coup many times.

'Why should I believe you?'

Teakettle shrugged.

'Why should I be here, otherwise? I am far from Apache tribal lands.'

'True. Have you other proof of what you say? What about this captain you claim as master?'

Teakettle's face flushed at the inferred insult. Scouting for the white men was looked down upon by Indians of all tribes. It was a betrayal of trust.

'The white chief is not my master. I serve the army for a purpose. I keep the Apache informed of the great white chief's plans. We can learn much of their tactics of war. May I know the name you are known by?'

The young Cheyenne threw up his head proudly.

'I am Tommy Eagle Eye, brother of Chief Kingfisher Blue.'

'So you too have a white man's name!' Teakettle made it sound derisory. The youth flushed.

'Not of my doing. I was called so by my father because a trapper called Tommy saved his life just before I was born,' he said hurriedly. 'So why are you spying and where is this troop of soldiers you speak of?'

'Have you no scouts ranging the hills? Surely you must be aware that there are soldiers nearby?'

Tommy Eagle Eye looked embarrassed.

'My chief has much on his mind. We are short of braves. We are not painted for war against the military. We are helping a white medicine man rescue his brother's wife and children. That man you seek kidnapped them and we are honour-bound to help this medicine man. Even now, our shaman is freeing her.'

'And how will he do that?' asked Teakettle curiously.

'There are many ways into the sacred Cave of the Skull that we Cheyenne know of.'

'Huh! So you think they will beat the water? They will get out?'

'You know about the water?'

'Of course. It is well known that when the water table rises, the water will flood underground tunnels and in this case make for the river. Only a fool would not know that!'

'So how do you expect to take this man you hunt, alive?'

Teakettle couldn't resist a grin. The tension had eased and he knew he was safe from this youth. They were speaking as man to man, not as captor and prisoner.

'My chief does not. He expects the Cheyenne to do the work for him.'

'And why should he?'

'There is a great price on his head, dead or alive. The great white chief sets much store on taking this man alive and he will be very grateful.'

Tommy Eagle Eye's eyes gleamed.

'You speak truth?'

'As I say, why should I be here if not to watch and wait?'

'Then I must go and report. We shall make sure we take that man alive. The white medicine man also wants him alive for killing his brother and taking his woman. *Ayeeha!* It is a good day today and the omens are auspicious. We shall get this man alive and punish him and only then can you have him!'

They stared at each other for several seconds, then Teakettle held out his hand, palm facing Tommy Eagle Eye. They slapped hands and grinned at each other. Then Tommy Eagle Eye turned and left Teakettle to crouch and watch and wait . . .

★   ★   ★

Cass Warton had watched the bunch of panicked horses erupt from the cave, knowing that Black Lynx must have freed them. The knowledge lifted his spirits, but he watched in horror at the sudden spurt of water from the cave entrance, and in his imagination he saw Black Lynx with Tim and Annie and the youngsters all swept away on a tidal wave.

His bowels turned to water. He gripped his rifle firmly. He'd never felt so ill even in his army days when he'd faced dealing with soldiers with horrific injuries.

Now he turned to Kingfisher Blue, white-faced and haggard.

'You think they will be in time to get out?'

Kingfisher Blue looked grim.

'It depends on the force of the water backed up in the passages. It is not yet running full. They have a good chance.'

In the next few hours, Cass repeated the chief's words to himself over and over again. He witnessed the straggly return of the horses and watched as rifles cracked and the men on horseback went down. For a while he was too busy himself for brooding on the fate of his brother's family.

There were milling horses in front of the cave, despite the stream of water gushing forth. The outlaws were using the horses as shields as the Indians on this side of the river took a dreadful toll of men and beasts.

There were screams and yells and some of the outlaws tried scrambling up the cliff face to get out of range of the pitiless onslaught. Bullets whined and spat, as men and horses fought to escape.

Then suddenly a great wall of water erupted from the cave itself and the remaining men and horses were engulfed. All firing ceased on the other side of the river as the Indians watched, marvelling at the Great Spirit's intervention. He had come to their aid. It was good.

Cass, shaken at the spectacle, collapsed behind the rock that was sheltering him. He was a man of medicine, not a soldier and now reaction was setting in. That, with the anxiety of not knowing what had happened to the little family, was too much. His head drooped. He was all in.

Then Kingfisher Blue was tapping him on the shoulder.

'Our work is not yet done, Magic Hands.'

Cass looked up, startled.

'What do you mean?' Then he saw Black Lynx standing beside him. His heart leapt at the sight of his grim face. 'Annie and the children? Are they safe?'

Black Lynx nodded.

'They are safe in our camp and the boy, Tim, is with them. He is one of us now, a Cheyenne and you can be proud of him!'

Cass had never given way to emotion since he was a lad of seven. Now he struggled to keep his composure but put a hand out to Black Lynx.

'I am forever in your debt.'

They looked at each other gravely, two medicine men of different cultures who had united their traditions and training to become friends and colleagues.

Kingfisher Blue watched them impatiently.

'Come. We are wasting time. The one you hunt is escaping. Already he is riding away along the river bank, deserting his men like the snake in the grass that he is, so Tommy Eagle Eye reports.'

'But he is on the other side of the river and it is now a torrent!' Cass pointed out. 'How can we catch him?'

'We follow the river and where the gorge narrows, there is already a rope bridge always maintained for the Cheyenne. We cross there. Tommy Eagle Eye is already riding towards it. We shall get your man, I promise you!'

Cass wearily pulled himself together. He was getting too old for these capers, but memory of his brother spurred him on. He would never rest easy until Mitch Delaney was captured and punished . . .

★　★　★

Mitch Delaney was frightened for the first time in his life. His shouted orders to the remaining men were being ignored. They were in a panic and as the bullets hummed and spat and the horses floundered and kicked out at each other, he made his mind up fast. He would get out before they were all picked off.

He saw horses scream and fall, legs kicking as they died. He saw his men firing wildly at targets they could not see and then flinging up their arms as they were slammed by lead bullets.

Quickly Mitch led forth his own horse, hidden away by itself for such a contingency as this. It was already saddled and the precious share of the payroll was in his saddlebags. He congratulated himself on his foresight that he might have to leave in a hurry. No one noticed him lead the horse away, then he was aboard, digging his heels into the horse's ribs and bending low as he tried to put as much distance as possible between himself and the river.

The going was soft, the rain now a drizzle, but soon he was wet and he cursed as the horse foundered on ground now turned to a quagmire.

Well away from the river he drew rein to give the horse a rest. He knew he must consider the beast's welfare, for he could not go far on foot with heavy saddlebags plus food and a canteen of water.

It was one of the tightest situations he'd ever been in. It made it worse to think it had all come about through his own mistake. He should never have held that military train up. He glanced at the overstuffed saddlebags. The very sight of them could be a danger if he ran into trouble.

Thank God he'd got away without being seen . . .

But sharp Indian eyes had seen him sneak away. Teakettle smiled at Tommy Eagle Eye, who'd returned after reporting to Kingfisher Blue, and they both watched his progress until he was hidden by a clump of stunted firs.

'So there he goes.' Tommy Eagle Eye laughed.

'He's heading for the desert. He'll not get far.'

Teakettle studied the youth.

'You know the country well?'

'I should do. My folks hid out there when I was a child, during the uprisings. It's Cheyenne stamping ground.'

'Then I'd best get back to my chief and tell him where this feller is headin'.'

'Not so fast, brother! You can have him after we've finished with him. Magic Hands wants him and what Magic Hands wants, he gets!'

'He must be some great chief, your Magic Hands?'

'He saved my brother's leg when he was but a youth, and has now saved my brother's squaw and her child. He is a great medicine man and Kingfisher Blue is in honour bound to help him.'

'What has this renegade major done to Magic Hands?'

'Killed his brother and kidnapped the man's wife and children, and it's my guess the woman has been repeatedly raped.'

Teakettle nodded his head.

'What d'you expect from white trash? They are less than animals. They also defiled your sacred caves.'

'Yes. Kingfisher Blue plans his own revenge for that crime. The man your chief hunts will cry out for death and he will not get it! This major will be tiring. He must spare his horse if he hopes to reach Mexico.'

Teakettle gave a grim laugh.

'We can take our time. He is goin' nowhere. I shall return to my chief and you will return to Kingfisher Blue and

Magic Hands and after you have settled your business with the rest of the white eaters of dung, you will no doubt take up the trail.'

'And your chief will follow?'

'Of course. But he will take his time. My chief believes in others doing the work!'

They reached out to each other and clasped hands, then they parted company and rode away.

★ ★ ★

Kingfisher Blue listened intently to Tommy Eagle Eye's report. Cass watched their faces, not being able to understand the language. He saw Kingfisher Blue's face tighten grimly. It looked like bad news.

The firing had ceased and now there was only the roar of water sweeping down into the gorge. There was still a waterspout coming from the sacred cave entrance but now Cass judged it to be not so fierce. But everything in that cave would be swept away.

'What is it?' he said finally as Kingfisher Blue turned to him.

'That mad dog got away. Tommy Eagle Eye saw him sneak away, but the good thing is that he was headin' for the desert. A day's ride and he'll be in dry country and there will be no going back for him.'

'So what do we do?'

'We follow of course. What else?'

'You think we can catch him?'

'It is only a matter of time. Already his horse will be blown and maybe lame. Remember the condition of the horse we found dead. Ridden hard with poor feed and very little rest. That renegade will never reach Mexico.'

'So perhaps we should let him go?'

Kingfisher Blue looked affronted.

'We catch and punish him even if we lose one of our young braves. It is a matter of honour!'

Cass rubbed the stubble on his chin. He would never understand the

Cheyenne reasoning. They would sacri-
fice one of their own, to fulfil a debt of
honour.

'Right! Then how do we get over the
river?'

'A half-day's ride up river and we
come to a rope bridge which has been
used for generations to get to the other
side.'

'How about the horses?'

Kingfisher Blue grinned.

'No problem. We take them over one
by one in a sling. How else?'

Cass shrugged. These Cheyenne had
answers for everything. It sure beat
going back out of the gorge and looking
for a fording place in the river,
especially now when it was in flood.

'You think your scouts will get on his
trail?'

Kingfisher Blue looked scornfully at
him.

'Of course. His trail will be a snake's
track, a blind man could follow it!'

Cass wasn't so sure. Kingfisher
sounded confident but Cass thought of

the hard ground that Delaney would deliberately choose, so as to leave as little evidence of his passing as possible. At least, that would be what he would do if he was Delaney.

He nodded.

'Well, I'm out of my depth here, Blue. It's up to you and your boys. All I want is to face him and beat shit out of him for my brother and what he did to Annie and the kids.'

Kingfisher Blue gave him a strange considering look and slowly shook his head.

'Is that all you want, Magic Hands? Don't you want to kill him? An eye for an eye? That is the law.'

'No, Blue. At first I wanted to kill him. That was a natural reaction, but then I remembered my oath. A doctor doesn't wantonly kill. He cures. Someone else will kill Delaney. I'm sure of that!'

They looked at each other and Kingfisher Blue got the message. He nodded slowly.

'It will be done.'

Kingfisher Blue went into frenzied action. He picked four of his best trackers, who included Tommy Eagle Eye. They packed the minimum of food but all carried parfleches, the useful skin bags that all Indians learned to make at an early age, now full of fresh clean water. They carried old army rifles and their own special knives, with which they excelled in one-to-one fighting.

They looked fierce and determined and Cass thanked God they were friends and not enemies.

Tim had returned to the war camp after seeing his mother and siblings settled. Now he rode beside his uncle. He'd matured in these last weeks and now reckoned he was a man, although he still had to count coup, as Tommy Eagle Eye explained that young braves must do. It was all so awesome. He shivered. It was all very well having a gun of his own, but would he have the nerve to face a man and shoot him? But thoughts of his mother and Jess and Bobby kept his anger simmering. The man they were now hunting was responsible. He hoped they would catch up with him quickly.

He glanced at his uncle and wondered what thoughts were going through his mind.

'Uncle . . . ' he began tentatively.

'Yes, Tim?'

'What will happen to Delaney?' He nodded at Kingfisher Blue and Black Lynx riding ahead.

Cass shook his head.

'Son, I shouldn't ask. All I know is that if we get hold of him I'd like to beat hell out of him. After that . . . ' He hesitated and shook his head again. 'Whatever happens I don't think we should interfere. These fellers have their own laws of punishment and execution.'

Tim looked solemn.

'He'll die, won't he?'

'Oh, yes, make no mistake about that; he'll die, but how I don't know.'

'Why will they be so set on killing him?'

'It's hard to understand the Indian mind, but part of it is that he's rampaged in their territory and partly it is because now we are Cheyenne, and so we must be avenged. We're blood brothers, remember, and will be all our lives. We play fair by them and we and our families will be protected by them. If we transgress . . . well, our punishment would be all the greater. You remember that all your life, Tim. We tread a fine line.'

Tim nodded and rode on. He had much to think about.

The sun had gone down when they reached the rope bridge. They had watched the gradual rising ground from the marshy plain in the canyon, and now it dipped again. The river was now slicing through another narrow gorge. The rope bridge had been fashioned at the point where the gorge was at its narrowest. Great tree trunks had been felled and rolled into place and the plaited ropes intertwined to make a swing-bridge. Rough branches had been interwoven with the rope for stepping on. To Tim's eyes it was like a horizontal ladder with ropes at each side for handholds.

At one side, there was a cage-like contraption with pulley ropes. He watched in wonder as the young braves seized each horse, harnessed it well into the cage of ropes and then all hauled together as the horse, squealing and kicking, was heaved over the river. Two youths walked the bridge and steadied the swinging cage. When they reached the other side they soon had the animal unhitched and tethered with a long rawhide rope to a sapling that grew several yards from the edge of the jagged rocks while one youth clambered back for the next beast.

Meanwhile, Kingfisher Blue motioned to Cass to take Tim across. For the first time in his life Tim had vertigo; his head swam and he wanted to vomit over the side.

Shakily he scrambled off the bridge and felt better on firm ground and joined the grinning youth left to watch the horses when they came across.

When all were over, Kingfisher Blue led them down the steep gradient to the valley below and announced that they would rest and eat and let their horses recover from their ordeal.

He pointed to a gap in the far hills.

'That is the only outlet from this end of the canyon and that is where we shall get on to Delaney's trail. I expect the scouts to return to us before morning to report on his condition and how fast he is able to travel. Meanwhile we shall rest and start again at dawn.'

The young braves soon had a fire going and they sang as they gathered wood. For them, it was a kind of recreational break from the humdrum chores of village life and there was always the excitement of the hunt. The songs they sang were of brave heroes who notched their coup sticks many times, killing both men and animals.

Cass and Tim watched and listened. At last the youth whom Tim had helped with the horses pulled him to his feet and Tim joined them in a dance.

'Why are they doing this?' asked Cass of Black Lynx, who smiled his slow grim smile.

'They ask blessings from the Great Spirit that all goes well with the hunt. They regard the man we hunt as an animal. To kill him will purify the earth. They all want to be part of the killing.'

Cass shuddered.

'He's a man, not an animal! I would wish that this man will be killed quickly.'

Black Lynx gave him a long contemptuous look.

'You are Cheyenne now. You must obey our rules.' He walked away before Cass could answer him.

That night, Cass's slumber was restless as he lay by Tim who hadn't moved once his blanket was around him. Cass wrestled with his conscience as a doctor and that of a man who'd lost his brother and wanted revenge.

He was up before dawn but not before Kingfisher Blue and his men. They were all out there, ready to greet the sun as it came up like a shining orb over the rim of the far hills, bathing the valley in a golden pink glow. Tommy Eagle Eye had come in during the night and confirmed a sighting of Delaney on a lame horse.

After a scanty breakfast of jerked meat and only water to drink, they set off snaking their way across the valley, led by Tommy Eagle Eye.

The hunt was on. The scent was fresh. It would only be a matter of time . . .

11

Mitch Delaney examined the swollen fetlock and cursed, running his hand over it and feeling the heat. What it wanted was cold running water to take down the swelling and from what he could see as far as the horizon there was nothing but desert scrubland dotted with stunted bushes and a sparse layer of brown sun-dried grass.

He straightened his back, removing his Stetson and wiped from his forehead the sweat that threatened to drip into his eyes.

He'd noted also that the shoe on that hoof was worn. He reached for his canteen and took a drink. The canteen was half empty. He didn't even have enough to share with the beast whose head was hanging low while its sides heaved.

It was a sorry-looking animal. Given

the choice of another mount he would have had no qualms in shooting it.

In his situation now, he needed it, half-dead as it was. He must walk. He couldn't risk his weight on it again until that swelling went down.

They both needed shelter, and quickly, as the sun would soon be at its zenith. He looked upwards: the sun was a brassy ball of heat. He swallowed. Already his throat was dry as if he'd never drunk.

He cursed that canyon and its only way out through that gap in the mountain range. He'd had no idea of the terrain he would enter. He'd expected low-lying grasslands, not this goddamned arid waste.

But he knew he was heading in the right direction. Mexico! All his troubles would be over once he crossed over the Rio Grande.

All he had to do was hole up somewhere and tighten his belt, get them both out of the goddamn sun and let the animal rest. If he foraged around during the coming night he might trap some small animal or even find a hidden waterhole.

He set his teeth, jammed his hat well down over his eyes, and taking the horse's bridle he led him, limping, forward towards a far distant cluster of rocks.

Much later, those rocks didn't seem any nearer. They were tantalizingly close, shimmering in the heat of the noonday sun. He licked dry and swollen lips and now his tight, high-heeled riding boots were making his feet swell. He limped nearly as much as the horse, which he was now having to haul after him.

He paused to take another swig from the canteen. Not enough to swallow but just to wet the inside of his mouth. A flicker of fear was now growing rapidly into full-blown panic. He was frightened as he'd never been in his life before. He'd faced bullets and hand-to-hand fighting with knives before, but then he'd had the strength to fight back. This menace was something he couldn't fight. He felt his strength and his will power seeping away and even his eyes were dimming.

He stoppered his canteen and carefully hooked it to his belt. It was the most precious thing he had in life. To the fortune in his saddlebags he paid no heed. What was a fortune anyway if he had no water?

He found himself staggering and holding on to the flagging horse. He knew he would have fallen to his knees if the animal hadn't been there . . .

Then suddenly he was conscious of a change of temperature. Looking up he saw that they were in the shadow of a looming rock. Dazedly he looked around. It had been hours since he had done that and was amazed to find that the cluster of rocks seen so far away were now within a hundred yards.

He straightened up and leaned away from the horse to see better. He blinked. Surely he was dreaming? The foliage at the foot of those rocks seemed to be greener than that growing near by. Was it because they grew in the shade?

He started to run, dragging the reluctant animal with him. Then, as they neared the rocks, the animal twitched his ears and his nostrils wrinkled. He gave a hoarse squeal and quickened his stride.

Water! Mitch Delaney's confused brain sent the word hurtling through his mind. Water! There must be goddamned water somewhere around, for the horse could smell it!

Both horse and man stumbled forward and there, in a tiny hollow below an outcrop of stone, was the muddy beautiful sight of a waterhole.

It was surrounded by many blurred footprints of all kinds of animals. It was perhaps ten feet across and in the middle of it was a puddle of thick soupy ochre-coloured water.

Sobbing with relief, Mitch Delaney threw himself into the sticky gooey mess. He reached out and drank the treacle-like liquid. It tasted acrid but it was water. Then he dowsed his hat deep into the mud and watched the thick mixture slowly fill the crown. He heaved himself back out of the glutinous mud and offered it to his horse.

Reaction set in and he collapsed by the edge of the pool. He lay quietly while the horse moved away and started pulling at the coarse grass growing near by. He must have slept, for suddenly he was awake, frightened that he was alone and on foot. But he saw with relief that the animal was still grazing near by. Even the horse wasn't a fool and would not leave this place.

He dowsed his head with what was left of the water in the canteen. He could now use an old army trick, learned from the Indians: how to filter the water from the mud. He knew that drinking it as it was would bring on the gripes. He would have to find lichen and devise a way of making a funnel and he would have to refill his hat. It would take time for the water to drip through the lichen, which would hold back most of the thick mud, and run clear, and it would have to run into his canteen . . .

He solved the problem by using his gun barrel after dismantling it and shoving one end into the canteen. The other end he bound with his neckerchief to one of his saddle-pouches in the bottom of which he gouged a hole. Then he painstakingly poured water from his hat into the pouch and watched anxiously for the water to seep through.

After a long agonizing wait, he heard the first drips hit the bottom of the canteen. He took a chance and poured the first spoonful on to his hand. It was nearly clear. He wet his lips with it. It was brackish but not salty. At that moment it was the most important thing in his world.

He laughed out loud and must have gone crazy; then he cried until he was exhausted.

Now his belly was rumbling. He must eat to keep up his strength. He must find food and as soon as possible. Already the shadows were lengthening. Soon it would be night, and then the nocturnal animals would come out. He would settle for a desert rat or a snake and he would eat it raw. No need to light a fire and alert anyone fool enough to be in this goddamned region.

He caught an unsuspecting baby jack rabbit intent on watching a movement in the grass. He had it by the ears before it was aware of danger. A sharp blow with the edge of his hand against its neck stopped its struggles. He took out his knife and slit its belly, his mouth watering at the sight of blood . . .

★   ★   ★

The young tracker called Bald Eagle, on account of losing a tuft of hair after an encounter with an eagle when out raiding birds' nests, sat his horse easily. He was doing two things. He was easing his back and he was allowing his pinto stallion, which was his pride and joy, to fill his belly while he had the chance. He was perched high on a grassy plateau overlooking what the Cheyenne referred to as the Devil's Strip.

He didn't expect to see much movement, but he knew that the man they hunted must pass this way if he was to make for Mexico. His keen eyes recorded all the details of the landscape. He noted the landfall and the way the ground gradually rose before coming to the far hills. He watched carefully each minute change in sunshine and shadow. No movement would escape him. He was trained to watch an area measured in his mind's eye before he moved on to the next area.

He saw a hawk rise and circle in the sky and watched it swoop and catch some bird in its talons and fly away. There was little else to see in the heat of the day.

Then, his legs spontaneously tightened about his mustang's belly. He had seen movement, a tiny dot with a larger dot behind it.

The movement was slow and laborious with many stops. If it hadn't been for the hawk swooping low he might have missed it. Bald Eagle smiled. There was no doubt. The dots were a man and a horse and the man was walking and hauling the horse behind him.

He squatted and lit the small fire of damp wood which he had ready for such a contingency as this. Blowing on the dry grass under the wood he fanned the flame until it took hold. It crackled and soon there was a plume of black smoke rising into the sky.

He watched the surrounding country and nodded as first one and then another plume of smoke arose. His job was done.

Then he saw a third plume away to the east and scowled. Someone else was out there watching and waiting for a message. He knew that none of his brother scouts would be in that area. It did not make sense. But it was none of his business. His chief would most certainly know who was out there . . .

★ ★ ★

Teakettle saw the smoke signal from high up in the hills and watched the two answering signals. So Kingfisher's men had located the man they all hunted. That was good. He sent his own message to Swift Deer, who would ride back to the troop. He watched his smoke rise into the sky, then he wheeled his horse and rode away. He would cut across the valley and intercept the troop as they neared their quarry.

★ ★ ★

Mitch Delaney had a full belly. He'd gorged himself on raw rabbit and never had bloody raw meat tasted so good. He belched and lay back against the rock which was still warm from the heat of the sun. If only he'd had coffee or, better still, a bottle of whiskey, he would have indeed been happy.

He blanked out the rigours to come. Sufficient unto the day, he thought and, for a moment, reality hit him; maybe he was going crazy, but no, he didn't feel crazy, just confident. Mitch Delaney's luck always held. He'd been in many tight spots in his turbulent life and he'd always managed to come out on top. He would best this cursed desert and enjoy the fruits of his labours.

He laughed when he thought of the fortune in his saddlebags. From the moment he hit Mexico it would be good food, women and as much liquor as he could drink. His future was a rosy-red glow.

He gave no thought to his men who'd followed him. They'd used him as he'd used them. There were no regrets about their deaths, not even of his most trusted lieutenants. He regretted the loss of the woman, but there would be others.

He frowned. The woman reminded him of the Cheyenne. Why would they be interested in the woman or the children? Dimly he remembered the attack, well organized and deliberate. He shook his head. He didn't want to remember the shock of that attack.

He reached for his canteen, lifted it and took a drink. It shattered in his hand, water spilling over him. He felt a stinging pain in his right hand.

He looked at his hand in shock. It dripped blood. He looked wildly around. Who in hell . . . ? Then he saw them. A row of heads looking down at him from above. The bastards had somehow climbed up behind him.

Sobbing, he scrambled to his feet and, conscious of soiled pants, he ran to his horse hobbled nearby. He took heart because apart from that one bullet there was no more firing. Frantically he freed the startled animal, climbed aboard and, digging his heels into the animal's ribs, lunged forward at a gallop.

He must have covered a hundred yards and was beginning to think that maybe he was going to get away. His fear turned to crazy exultation. Lady Luck was with him despite the wounded hand.

Then came the rifle bullet which hit the horse's rump and a split second later the horse squealed and fell, Delaney heard the explosion. He cursed as he rolled and hit the ground. Whoever the bastard was, he was a cool devil, deliberately waiting and giving him, Delaney, hope that he would escape.

He was lying on his back, winded, eyes staring, when Cass Warton peered down at him.

'Get up! I'm going to give you the hidin' of your life!'

Mitch Delaney raised himself on his elbows.

'What you talkin' about, man? What have I done to you?'

'Remember that homesteader you killed and the woman and kids you took after you burned the homestead to the ground?'

'What of them?' Mitch Delaney licked dry lips.

'He was my brother and the woman and kids all the family I've got. I'm takin' it out of your hide, Delaney!' With which Cass grabbed Delaney by the throat and heaved him to his feet. With the other hand he punched him in the belly. 'That's for starters!'

Then Delaney shook his head and, ignoring the pain in his hand, went into a crouch. From a sheath hanging from his trouser belt he whipped out a knife and lunged at Cass. But Cass was ready for him and leapt aside, catching Delaney a blow in the neck.

Then the real battle commenced. Several cuts later, Cass managed to grip the wrist that held the knife; then they were swaying and jabbing and gouging and both took painful blows to the groin.

Around them stood Tim and King-fisher Blue and Black Lynx and one of the trackers. Tim wanted to rush forward and help his uncle when Cass was on his back and it looked as if Delaney might choke him.

Kingfisher Blue held him back.

'Wait! This is not your fight. Your uncle's honour is at stake. He will not want your help. He must do it alone!'

The Cheyenne stood impassively as the fight raged on. Sometimes it was Cass who was the stronger, sometimes it was Delaney, despite his wounded hand. It made him fight all the more fiercely until both men were covered in blood.

Then Cass whipped the knife away and caught Delaney a glancing blow on the side of the head which made him stagger back. Then Cass's piledriver came up and connected to his chin. It flung him up into the air and he hit the ground with a sickening thud. He lay still and Cass staggered back, suddenly drained of strength.

Tim rushed forward and caught him as he swayed.

'You all right, Uncle?'

'Yes, boy. Give me a few minutes. I'll be fine.'

'I'll help you mop the blood, Uncle.'

'It's all right, boy. I'll do the necessary. Just you hang around.'

Cass suddenly sat down. His head hung down and he passed a weary hand over his eyes. Then he looked up at Tim.

'What are they doin' with Delaney?'

Tim looked around and saw the young scout dragging Delaney's body by the heels to a sheltered spot amongst the rocks.

'They're dragging Delaney away, Uncle. The chief and Black Lynx look mighty strange, like they've changed into wild animals. I'm frightened, Uncle Cass!'

'You stay by me, boy and close your ears as well as your eyes. It's not somethin' you should witness.'

'What they goin' to do, Uncle?'

Cass did not answer but pulled Tim down beside him.

★   ★   ★

Mitch Delaney opened his eyes and groaned. He ached all over and his head felt like it was busted. He looked up at Black Lynx who was crouched down rubbing oil into his body, which he saw now was naked.

'What are you gonna do with me?' he croaked.

Black Lynx laughed showing a set of fine teeth, except for the two front ones which had been knocked out in a traditional ceremony when he was a boy.

'Oil makes meat cook better. It seals the juices in. You must know that.'

Mitch Delaney's eyes opened wide and threatened to jump from their sockets. Shocked, he nearly choked as he vomited.

Black Lynx sprang back to miss the issuing mess.

'Now where is all the white man's courage you show when surrounded by your men? Where is the arrogance that lets you raid our villages and rape our women and kill our old men and children, eh?'

He bent low again to stare Delaney in the face. He spat on him. 'You walk under snakes, you live in slime like a dung beetle!'

Angered, Delaney lifted his leg and caught Black Lynx a vicious kick in the chest.

Then Black Lynx moved swiftly. He heaved Delaney up from the ground and threw him to his young scout, who grinned and threw him back again as if he was a bundle of rags. The game went on until Delaney's head fell forward and his eyes closed and they tired of the game.

Then Kingfisher Blue was there beside them. He had organized a fitting place for Delaney, a gathering of wood had been built into a cone-shaped pile between two jagged needles of rock. A rope was now attached to the rocks and, at a gesture, Mitch Delaney's body was dragged to it and he was suspended by the rope above the firewood, his legs stretched wide and weighted by heavy rocks on each side of the cone.

It was the smoke and heat that brought Delaney to his senses again. He moved his head and saw that his arms were stretched out and roped and his legs opened as wide as they would go and it was a smouldering fire beneath his balls that was sending fire through him.

He screamed as the fire licked at the oil on his legs and genitals and slowly crept upward, so that his body became a mass of flame. His hair and beard caught fire and he writhed and strained at his bonds, and all the while the screaming went on.

Cass's head cleared at the sound. He held Tim down so that he couldn't see, although no matter how the boy stuffed his ears, he couldn't blot out the sound.

Cass stood upright and moved closer,

gripping his rifle. He saw the stationary Cheyenne watching without emotion. The bastards weren't men as he knew them. They were demons. He wanted to be sick. No man or animal should be subjected to what Delaney was going through, no matter how evil he was.

Slowly Cass lifted the rifle. He knew what he had to do. It went against his oath as a doctor to deliberately kill in cold blood. But he had to do it.

He heard Tim sobbing behind him. This was something the boy should never have had to witness.

He took careful aim. It would have to be one shot before those demons knew what he was about. Then he pulled the trigger and the report echoed far and wide. He saw Delaney's face explode into a blood-red mass; the screaming ceased and there was a silence which hurt the ears.

Then Cass threw down the rifle and went to Tim and held him close.

'It's all over, Tim. We can go home to your ma.'

Later, Kingfisher came to stand before him, face grave and sorrowful.

'You interfered, Magic Hands. Why? He was a bad man.'

'He'd suffered enough, Blue.' Kingfisher Blue shrugged.

'You white-eyes are hard to understand. You are capable of great cruelty and yet you are also capable of compassion. You are hard to understand, Magic Hands.'

Cass smiled.

'You too are hard to understand. Maybe, someday, we shall find a common meeting ground and our differences will be ironed out. It might come in the boy's time. I don't know.'

They smiled at each other.

'Meanwhile, you will help us, Magic Hands? Black Lynx is eager to learn from you.'

'It's a start, Blue. Perhaps that is the way to a better way of helping each other.' He glanced at the body of the man who'd been responsible for the death of his brother and the harrowing ordeal of Annie and her children. 'What of him? Do we bury him?'

Kingfisher Blue looked affronted.

'We do not soil our hands or expend our energy on such as he. We leave him to the buzzards!'

'We can't do that, Blue. He's entitled to a burial.' Blue shrugged.

'You shot him. You bury him!' Then his face creased into an unaccustomed grin. '*Aaeeah!* My scout will return him to his own people. He knows where the white-eyes troop are heading. Yes, that would be fitting, Magic Hands?'

Cass nodded. It seemed right and proper for a renegade officer to be returned and disposed of by the military . . .

* * *

Teakettle, with Swift Deer flanking the column, drew his mustang to an abrupt halt. He shaded his eyes as he saw movement in the far distance.

Captain Plumpton, with his sergeant

219

heading the column, saw the gesture and raised his arm to halt his men. His eyes raked the terrain in front of him but he only saw the hazy blue-grey misty hills and the burning ochre arid land which he hated.

'Call Teakettle over, Sergeant, and find out what's bothering him,' he ordered peremptorily. He was nervous. His skin crawled. Out in the open, his nerves screamed. He expected an arrow in his back at all times.

Bill Steel's lips curled. God knows what would happen to the captain if they were ever attacked by the red men. He called Teakettle over.

'What is it, Teakettle?'

Teakettle did not answer but pointed. Bill Steel shaded his eyes from the glare and studied the terrain. Then catching his breath he rode back to the captain.

'Sir, one rider coming lickety-split. It appears he's come through the pass. Shall we ride on to meet him or wait?'

The captain grunted. His arse ached

and he wanted to urinate but for once thought it best to appear to be in command.

'We ride on and meet whoever's in such a hurry.' His arm came up automatically and the troop moved on.

A half-hour later they could see that it was an Indian. It was Teakettle who recognized him as Kingfisher Blue's scout and he guessed the contents of the wrapped tarpaulin that lay slung in front of the rider.

Then, when the horse and rider were within a hundred yards of the troop, the captain raised his arm to stop.

It seemed to the watching men that the Indian increased his speed and came to a halt in a spectacular rearing of his mount. Then with a heave of bulging muscles the tarpaulin-wrapped parcel was flung on the ground in front of his horse. The rider then reared again and, turning swiftly without a look or a word, galloped back the way he had come.

Captain Plumpton looked at the still

package and then at the Sergeant.

'D'you think it's what I think it is, Sergeant?'

'Only way to find out, sir, is to take a look.'

'Then do it, Sergeant.'

A few minutes later, Bill Steel looked at the bloodied face of the man they had been hunting. The hunt was over.

★　★　★

Annie Warton never recovered from her ordeal. She became a recluse on the ranch, always frightened of white strangers who might visit.

Cass Warton found that his duty lay with the Indians. He built a small log cabin beside the main ranch house and made his home there, for later, with the help of Tim and some of the Cheyenne, he built a small clinic which eventually expanded into a makeshift hospital.

Five years later Tim left to go East after helping his uncle in the hospital.

He knew he wanted to be a doctor like his uncle.

Bobby grew up and took over the ranch and looked after Annie in her declining years.

Jess never married. She became a nurse to the Cheyenne and later to the white settlers in the small towns that were now springing up.

Kingfisher Blue's family increased and he never forgot his debt to Magic Hands.

Black Lynx learned much from Magic Hands and worked with Cass for many years. They became great friends as well as colleagues.

Sometimes, when Cass sat on his own veranda at night, watching the sun set and smoking his pipe, he would ponder how fate and the murder of his brother Steve had helped to shape his future and that of Tim of whom he was so very proud.

Yes, good had sprung from something bad. He would always grieve for Steve and for poor Annie who had gone

through so much. But life had to go on
and there were so many folk, both red
and white to help. He knew his place in
the scheme of things . . .

THE END

STONE MOUNTAIN

Concho Bradley

The stage robbery had been accomplished by an old woman. Twine Fourch had never heard of a female being a highway robber before. He followed the trail all the way to a dilapidated log cabin up Stone Mountain. What happened after that no one could believe even after townsmen from Jefferson found the old log house and the skeletal dying old woman. But before the mystery could be solved there would be two unnecessary killings, a bizarre suicide and a lynching.